KING & QUEEN

RELIC # 3

MAZ MADDOX

Maz Maddox ♡

Content Edited by Raven Max

To my betas: Katie, Maira, Amy and Angela. Thank you for always helping make my story the best it can be.
And a special thanks to Rebecca for being my awesome sensitivity reader! Thank you for your valuable feedback and perspective.

CHAPTER ONE

ROYAL

Late spring mornings were my favorite.

The dew across the tall grass was cold against my hide; birds sang sleepy songs to the soft morning sunlight. The smell of earth and growth was all around, much more crisp and cool than they used to be. Even though it was a little too chilly for me, I still enjoyed our morning rituals. My herd was scattered out, hunting, roaming, stretching their legs before the day began.

I shut my eyes as I breathed in deep, my frill catching the warmth of the sunlight dripping in past the horizon.

Peaceful. Calm.

I smelled him long before I could see him. Stalking the tree line to my right, a predatory shadow had his eyes locked on me. I kept my pace, easy and calm, never alerting him that he had been found out. A long time ago in another life, if I had known there was a threat lurking in the edges of my territory, I would immediately call out to my herd. My bellowing cry would direct the bulls to surround the calves, horns out and ready to defend.

But not now. My herd didn't need protection against this one.

And he wasn't going to win anyway.

Through the tall grass, he crept low and steady, aiming for my haunches. It would be stupid to try anything else, considering my horns were sharp and could go through the side of a car door. My frill, which I was very proud of, was the perfect bone shield to keep assholes from biting my neck. So the only play they had was to attack from behind.

Life always underestimated how fast big guys could move. I was big, and I was fucking fast.

When he finally sprang, I caught him mid-air with my tail. I spun to the side, knocking him backwards by the throat before facing him with my horns. He staggered back across the grass but sprang back up to launch a full-frontal attack. I ducked my head to take the brunt of his weight with my frill instead of my horns, so I didn't stab him in the damn chest.

I grunted and threw him off, pretending to yawn.

Dalton hissed and splayed his black tail feathers in a mocking gesture. Cocky raptor asshole.

Yeah, it's all fun and games until you get a horn in the ass.

I tilted my horns down again, openly challenging him. The bright pink feathers on Dalton's head rose like an aggravated cockatiel, flaring to life as he flexed his claws. I sidestepped as he did. The slow circle we traced made the wet grass tickle my sides. He tried to fake to the right before dipping off to the left, leaping to try and grab onto my side. I charged forward, slamming my wide frill into his side and sending him back into the grass.

I gave him another huff, trotting in a slow circle to let him know I was making fun of him. He deflated his pink feathers and sneezed some wet grass out of his nose. He rose to his feet to begin again when the massive shadow of a much, *much* bigger predator paused our fun.

Leader. Big brother.

Dalton and I turned towards the massive T.rex watching us, the morning sunlight mostly blocked by his large body. If he wasn't herd, wasn't family, I would be running as fast as I could. As previously mentioned, I was pretty damn fast, but he was faster. His jaws would have crushed my bones. My frill would be snapped and broken under his teeth. There was no way I could win against Montana.

But we weren't going to fight. He was herd. My herd.

He lifted his nose and smelled the air, considering it a moment before turning back towards the house. It was time to go inside. Our morning exercise was over. Dalton darted forward to race for the massive sail on Baha's back, which I could see lumbering towards the house. I fell in line beside Montana, giving a huff when I heard Baha's "it's too early for your bullshit" hiss he gave the bouncing Utahraptor at his side.

Overhead, Jackson's wingspan cast long shadows over us as he dipped down for a landing. The only non-dinosaur in the herd, and a new addition, Jackson had started joining our mornings when Baha wasn't shacked up at his ranch.

Another tyrannosaur was already ahead of us, smaller than Montana, with brilliant white feathers on his head catching the blood-orange of the sunrise. Yu looked back towards us, watching our motley crew of a herd moving together.

I was glad we were all together this morning. I loved mornings with my brothers.

Simon, the only human among us and Dalton's sweet, paleontologist boyfriend, always watched us in the mornings. Well, up until we shrank back down into our human forms. Then he politely excused himself from the naked men taking in the sunrise. Dalton would typically chase after him while the rest of us went for food.

It was crazy and unconventional, but it was us. And I loved it.

I pulled on some track pants and my favorite hoodie, heading for the kitchen to find something to eat.

"I need to talk to you in the briefing room," Montana informed me as I was leaning into the fridge.

"No time for breakfast?" I paused while pulling out the eggs. "I was gonna make omelets."

"After." Montana didn't leave room for argument, as always, and didn't glance back as he left the kitchen. Dalton moved past, only wearing boxers, and tossed me strawberry Pop-Tarts.

"He ate a deer while we were out," he said around a bite of his far inferior blueberry ones.

"Figures." I took a big bite of the processed sugar delicacy and scrolled through social media. The rest of my family might have been stuck in prehistoric times, but I sure as hell wasn't. I loved technology, loved computers specifically, and like all good (millions year old) Millennials, I lived on the damn internet. Dalton craned his neck over to look at my screen, licking icing off his lip.

"Your feed is all dicks and dinos."

"No it's not," I snorted, scrolling one flick down before angling my screen his way. "I got boobs and botanicals too. I'm a man of complex taste."

"I think they call that being a pansexual disaster."

"Nah. I'm a pansexual storm. Watch out because I'll blow you away."

Dalton, who was a man of culture, slapped his palm against mine as I held up my hand. Baha called us both fucking idiots as he passed us. It was a normal morning in the RELIC house. Dalton peeled off to no doubt cause mayhem as I met up with Montana in the briefing room.

I fell into the chair at the large table in the center of the room. The massive dining area in our large home had long ago been converted to our mission table. My computers were behind us where I spent most of my time hunting fossils, snagging intel, and finding the best memes on earth. When my ass wasn't parked in that chair, I was training hard in our gym, sparring with Montana or Yu, or setting up pranks with Dalton.

The latter had recently been cut back since he brought Simon home. I loved the guy, but he was really cutting in on my "fuck with everyone" time.

"Royal." Montana's voice pulled me from my screen. I lifted my chin to let him know I was listening. He shut the door to the meeting room, and I perked my eyebrows.

"What's up, boss?"

"I found two new fossil sites that need investigating." Montana opened up his laptop and passed it over to me. "One is in southeastern France. The other is in Alberta. Both have been yielding some interesting finds lately, and we need to scope them out."

"Scope them out for poaching threats?" I scanned over the pictures of the sites before glancing up. "Or do you think there's someone like us waiting under the rocks?"

Montana's visits to fossil sites only had two real motives. Either there was a tip off that a site was easy prey for fossil thieves, and he wanted us to keep them safe, or there was a sleeping beauty lying just below the surface.

It was much, much better if another shifter was there to welcome you to a world sixty-five million years in the future. Otherwise it's a little jarring. Not to mention having never seen a human before and waking up as one is pretty terrifying.

I would know.

"Both."

"Damn." I grinned. "That's kind of exciting. It's been what, forty years or so since you found Dalton and me? We could use some younger blood around here."

"Nothing is for sure yet. These scouting trips take time and patience. Usually, I come home with new contacts and information, not another shifter."

"Oh, no. *Only* new contacts and information from a cool part of the world? Poor you." I scrolled through the information he had on both sites, the lead paleontologists working it, finds so far, and so on. "So, which one are you heading to first? I can get to work setting up a network and pulling info for you. Need a new passport?"

"Is yours up to date?" Montana crossed his arms, leaning his hip against the table.

"Mine?" I narrowed my eyes and uncurled from over the laptop. "You want me to go with you this time?"

"No. I want you to visit the site in Alberta while I go to France."

I scoffed a laugh because I knew he had to be joking. "Montana."

"All of the Cretaceous formations sites I found you and your brothers in had small, early mammalian ancestors findings. Both sites have been finding caches of small bones lately. The site in Alberta isn't far from where I found you."

I clicked over to the beautiful, sandy striped cliffsides that made up the countryside of Alberta. The ridgeline Montana had found me in was similar but with more grass topping the outcrop. Even though I had made my home in Texas with my brothers, I always had a soft spot for Alberta and its banded cliffs.

It was my stomping ground for most of my life. I guess, in a way, it was like my hometown, even if the tectonic plates had shuffled around quite a bit since then.

"I don't think I'm qualified to handle this kind of job." I leaned back in the chair to look at Montana again. "I'm the Guy in the Chair, boss. I'm support, the IT guy, the hot Black hacker who makes y'all's lives easier. I'm definitely not the guy who should be in charge of handling a freaked-out, groggy shifter coming to life after millions of years."

"I disagree," he said casually with a shrug. "I think you're very capable of handling this."

I gave him a leveling stare. "You base this on what? What in my skillset I just mentioned makes you think I can handle the fragile psychology of a prehistoric animal waking up as a sentient being?"

Montana smirked. "You're patient, kind and brilliant. And you know very well I can't send Dalton or Baha."

"Why not?" I laughed around my question because I knew damn well why not. Dalton would drag the poor person around Canada looking for something to set on fire, and Baha would probably leave it at a gas station somewhere. "I feel like they build character."

"It's unlikely there will even be a shifter under the rocks, Royal. Like I said, this is likely just going to be an intel assignment. But I want one of us there, just in case."

I rubbed both hands over my face and looked at the screen again. A blanket of prickling anxiety draped itself over my back as I stared at the Drumheller cliffs.

"I really prefer to stay with the herd, boss. I don't like traveling when you or anyone else is on a mission. What if you need my help?"

"I'll be alright. Dalton is going out with Simon on a camping trip, and Baha is still recovering from his last mission. Yu is heading back out to Japan, but he can tap you for intel if he needs it. You don't need to worry about your brothers or me."

It was annoying how well he could use logic against me. He was right, as he usually was. But it still made me feel like I swallowed a rock. Travelling for missions always made me uneasy, but this took the cake. Being that far away from everyone *and* possibly in charge of a new recruit was asking a hell of a lot.

But what else could I do? Let my brother down?

"Alright," I said reluctantly. "But if someone does wake up while I'm there, I'm teaching them nothing but cuss words the entire way back home. It'll be a cuss-a-saurus, and I'm not helping you fix it."

Montana chuckled. "Deal."

CHAPTER TWO

BLAISE

I was going hoarse from screaming over the bar.

This far into the night, the music at the club swallowed my voice before it could fly more than an inch from my lips. The bartender leaned over the slick countertop, tilting his ear my direction so I could try again. My third attempt at screaming my drink order was finally understood, and he nodded before bellowing out the price tag.

Ouch. This place was going to devour my very limited funds, but how often was I in downtown Calgary? Let's be real, all gay bars with speakers that loud were expensive, no matter where you were. Thank God I had everything else locked down on a tight budget. Tonight was drinks and dancing.

I deserved it. It had been an overwhelmingly shitty week.

It had taken almost everything I had to make it to Calgary, my hotel room charged me extra fees that wouldn't be returned for a damn week, and I wasn't even at my final destination yet. I still had a long drive out to Drumheller tomorrow to get to the fossil site. But this volunteer dig would be worth it. Being the first to stream the findings out there was going to get my boost my platform needed.

But that was tomorrow's problem.

My problem tonight was getting heard over loud music and finding someone to grind against.

The bartender passed over my drink, and I waved for him to keep the change after I handed over the bill. I thought I'd at least get a smile for the generous tip, but he took it without even nodding a thanks.

Rude.

The punch of alcohol I got from taking a gulp made me cough. Okay. At least I got my money's worth.

The pulsing music swirled into something with a heavy beat; the spinning lights swam over writhing bodies melting together. It was a sea of skin: toned arms, some abs, flashes of teeth and laughing mouths. It used to be so easy for me to slip into the ocean and find a partner, press myself into the madness and pick out a thrill. For some reason, my will to dive in had ebbed back as I watched the crowd.

Maybe I was getting too old for the club scene. I was nearing the end of my twenties, and it wasn't a cute look to be the almost thirty-year-old twink at a gay bar.

Some guys can pull it off. I just looked tired.

Glam as hell with killer cat eye, but still tired.

Tired twenty-something twink. That was my brand, I guess.

I was musing the idea of either buying another overpriced punch of vodka or heading home when a voice cut through the noise like a hot knife through butter.

"I like your necklace."

I blinked towards the masculine rumble that was near me, hoping it was aimed at me and not someone standing close by. Much to my surprise, he was grinning at me.

And the man was hot as fire.

Tall, brawny, rich ebony skin that was dark against his pale pink shirt that strained over his chest like it was painted on. His hair was a faded cut along the sides but just long enough on top to keep the style modern. The faint scent of a crisp cologne danced over him as he leaned in to speak over the music.

"I said I like your necklace," he said again, assuming I couldn't hear him over the blasting music.

I touched it as I answered like an idiot. "Thanks, it's a triceratops."

His teeth flashed as he smiled, amusement sparkling in his brown eyes. "I know."

You're a dumbass, Blaise.

It was then I noticed his obscenely loud hoodie he was wearing unzipped over his pink shirt. The hooded sweatshirt had tiny, pixelated, neon hearts, stars and dinosaurs all over it with the color scheme that could only be described as a 90's Chuck E. Cheese arcade floor. It was...not my style. Hell, I don't think it's *anyone's* style, but it fit him somehow.

I coughed, trying to ignore the heat rushing to my cheeks. "Um, want a drink?"

"That's my line." He lifted his chin to the bartender, his voice heard clearly the first time. "Another round and two shots." He looked my way. "What shot do you want?"

I bit my lip. "A royal fuck?"

The grin that man gave me melted my bones. "That can be arranged." His eyes scanned over me before going back to the bartender. "Two royal fucks."

I finished my drink so I would be ready for the next one and to help coax myself into being charming. The bartender passed along the shots, and I lifted mine the same time he did. I openly watched his mouth as he pulled his lips back into a smirk as our glasses touched. I tossed mine back, the icy blast against the back of my throat a welcome cooling sensation over the burning of my skin. I could feel his eyes on me, and I made a show of lapping up an imaginary drop from my lip.

When he took my hand and pulled me onto the dance floor, I didn't hesitate to follow. Now that I had a very fine shark leading me into the sea of bodies, I was happy to dive in. Moving against him, I let his much larger form swallow me whole. Pulses of light painted him in flashes, making the entire experience feel like a damn fever dream.

Like a pieced-together wet dream, I caught snapshots of the delicious man who was dancing with me. Thick chest, full lips, wide hands ghosting my hips before tugging me flush against him. The smell of his cologne mixed with the heady smells of sweat and alcohol, the lingering bite of someone smoking a candy-flavored vape.

My belly was warm with alcohol and lust, my neck tingling as his breath danced over my skin. His skin was hot against my fingers as I touched him, pushing under his shirt to touch his stomach. When I tilted my chin up to look at him, I loved that he was taller than me. I loved that he could probably snap me like a candy cane if he wanted to.

Fuck I wanted him to.

My mental broadcast was received, and I was pulled deeper into the darkness of the club. Off the floor, out of the sea, and into the blissful void.

The dark pockets of the building had other couples finding solace in the shadows, but there was still space to claim for ourselves. My back was pressed into the wall, my sight drowned out by the massive man in front of me. He hummed into my mouth as I tugged him closer by his ugly sweatshirt, his lips sweet from the shots as I sucked on them.

His moans travelled through me like liquid fire, burning every inch of me from the inside out. I had never been such an uncoordinated harlot in my life as I struggled to unzip his jeans. It had been a long time since I had a fling and even longer than that since I was this slutty in a club. I thought I had hung up my club-fucking days when I was still sneaking in with fake IDs.

But when was I going to get this kind of chance again? A guy like this never bought me drinks. A huge, hot mountain of a man wasn't the type that dished out dick to a guy like Blaise Fite.

So, yeah. He could fuck me in a dark corner of a club and never see me again.

Not surprising, the hot stranger was also hung like a goddamn bull. The moment he popped loose from the confines of his jeans, the damn thing nearly gave me a black eye. It was probably a fantastic ego boost that I had to push him further back so I could go down to my knees, but the guy was probably used to it. He no doubt got whoever he wanted with as fine as he was.

I made sure to let him know how *deeply* I appreciated his body. By the way his fingers dug into my scalp and tugged, I was worshiping him just right. The musky scent of his skin was likc no drug I had ever felt. The pressure down my throat of swallowing him burned just right.

It was the most debauched thing I had ever done, but holy hell was it amazing. The finishing blast down my throat choked me, but not so badly that it killed the mood. I was painfully aware my mascara was smudged from the tears, and the little bit of drool that fell down my chin wasn't exactly attractive.

I was tugged up to my feet in a daze, drunk on the heat of the moment and loose from the strain of holding my breath. When I was spun around, I almost tripped and braced myself against the wall as a wide palm dove under my waistband. I was so far beyond being subtle that I pushed my ass back against him as he manhandled me. His warm fingers tugged me loose from my jeans, stroking me in strong, smooth movements that made my knees buckle.

My body was already electric from the rough blowjob that I wasn't going to take much to make me pop. He knew that and made sure I felt every precious moment. While one hand stroked me, the other slipped up my shirt to thumb my nipple. His teeth nipped my ear, hot breath panting, his hips bucking into mine.

The thread holding me together snapped, my eyes flicking back with the thumping blasts of blinking lights behind my eyelids.

I came with a shout and a long whine of happiness.

If I could have crumbled onto the floor and rested without getting something truly revolting on me just then, I would have. My bones had turned to putty. My body was floating on orgasmic bliss. The stranger at my back the only thing grounding me.

When I felt his grip release me, reality slowly washed away the floating dream like a gentle tide.

I turned and rested back against the wall, smiling up at him as I adjusted everything back into place.

"That was fun."

"Yeah," he breathed with a grin. "Goddamn you are hot as hell like that."

"Freshly fucked and kinda drunk?" I winked, wiping some sweat from my face. He hummed in acknowledgement. "You wanna meet up again sometime?"

"I'm just passing through." He zipped himself up. "Just visiting Canada a bit before I head back to the US."

You knew this was a one-time thing, Blaise. Be happy it was fun.

"Sure." I shrugged. "It was nice meeting you anyway."

He didn't respond, only smirked and disappeared into the darkness of the club.

I didn't catch his name, and I knew I'd never see him again, but I wasn't going to forget the hot guy in Calgary any time soon.

Especially not that hideous fucking sweater.

"I'm sorry, if you're not a volunteer, you can't be out at the site."

This was not how I planned my afternoon to go. It had taken me hours to get out to the dig site, including a very long drive from Calgary, getting lost, and then hiking my happy ass out to the wilderness to find this place. I was sweaty from the long trip, tired and ready to finally get some pictures of the fossils that had been slowly excavated over the past year.

It didn't help that I was mildly hungover from my heathen evening in the city.

The new site from the Royal Tyrrell Museum was a treasure trove of new Cretaceous discoveries, and I wanted to be the first one to snap some exclusive shots. My plan had been to interview the paleontologists, the volunteers, and maybe do a livestream while I was out there for bonus exposure.

I even wore my new, super-cute fossil scarf for just that reason. Well, for the livestream and to keep the sun off of my neck. It's not a good look to be burned to a crisp while chatting up people.

"I was told that I was going to be added to the volunteer roster. I drove here from British Colombia. Could you double check?" I flashed my smile, hoping it was dazzling and charming, not exhausted and sweaty. "I wanted to see what the newest finds were and chat with the volunteers."

"Are you with the press?" The older gentleman adjusted his baseball cap on his head, sweeping his eyes over me skeptically. His gaze landed on my "I Dig Diversity" button in my jacket, a rainbow-colored strata with cartoon fossils buried inside.

He also didn't seem amused that I was wearing one of my favorite skirts. In my defense, it was extremely comfortable and adorable. It was a very breezy, light fabric with an open panel up the side and was perfect for long walks. I always paired it with some shorts under it in case the wind wanted to give away my business.

"I'm a Science Communicator and dinosaur enthusiast," I explained, leaving out the "aspiring" from my professional label. Sure, I hadn't been officially picked up by any museums yet, but that's why I was out there. Being able to approach a museum about my skills as a social media marketing expert and science communicator with a somewhat spontaneous visit out to Drumheller was exactly what I needed.

But Old Ballcap wasn't having it. His face didn't mask the unimpressed skepticism that floated to the surface as I explained myself. There was no doubt in my mind that this guy not only didn't know what a "Science Communicator" really was, but probably had his grandkids help him set up his Wi-Fi.

"If you're not with the group, you need to go, please." He pointed back the way I came. "We can't have people coming through here to post on Facebook."

"That's not at all what I'm doing," I tried, following him as he turned away. "I'm here to help communicate the amazing work the volunteers and paleontologists are doing out here to the general public. Think about it. If more people knew about the site, you might get more funding."

"No, thank you." He glanced over his shoulder. "Goodbye."

I sighed and slowly stopped following him, not wanting to

push him to the point of calling someone to escort me away. Scattered out in front of me was the site, a couple of tents set up to keep the volunteers safe from the sun as they chipped away at the rocks, hunting for fossils and other ancient forms of life. Just beyond a steep dip in the formation, I could see the clear signs of a big dig, lots of people milling around and setting up casting for large bones.

So close. Yet, so far.

I tried to zoom in with my digital camera that was hanging around my neck, but the incline made it impossible to really see. Damnit. I glanced towards where Old Ballcap had retreated and noticed he was still keeping an eye on me.

I forced a smile and gave a wave.

Yeah, fuck you too.

The hike back to Drumheller was very long and disappointing. The couple of shots I was able to sneak in while I was out there were grainy and boring. The landscape of the area was beautiful, don't get me wrong, but it wasn't going to get my platform any attention. Not only did I want to boost my ability to be seen as a proper science communicator, but I also desperately wanted to see the site.

The entire reason I became involved in science communication was because of my love for paleontology. I wanted to see cool dinosaur bones just as much as I wanted to further my career. What had they found? Was it something new? Something big and badass that'd end up across *Nature* and *National Geographic*?

Please be a new ceratopsian or sauropod. Theropods are so last year.

Drumheller itself was not a big town, but it was one of the most wonderfully ridiculous places I had ever been. The town was flanked by the same massive, banded cliffs as before, making the whole area feel like it was half submerged inside of a mountain. This paired with the town's aesthetic really made this place a unique, geological dream.

Everything was dinosaur themed: from the street names to the bright colorful fiberglass dinosaurs that decorated most businesses. I had seen pictures of this place, but none of them could do Drumheller true justice.

Anyone who even remotely loved dinosaurs had to visit at least once. It's a true Mecca for dinosaur nerds of all qualifications.

Since I had spent most of my money actually getting to Alberta, I had to go extra cheap for my accommodations. The listing on Airbnb said the building was a "charming little oasis near thriving tourist locations." What it should have said was "the apartment above a closed pharmacy that was the size of a closet."

It was cheap, in the heart of downtown, which meant I could get to places easily, and I could see a cute Brontosaurus sitting on a bench from my window. So, I only bitched a little bit when I had finally made it there after my long trip from Calgary. After a quick shower with lukewarm water, I crawled onto the bed which was tucked against the back wall. The ancient quilt spread over the queen mattress smelled a little stale, but it was shockingly comfortable.

I went through my pictures again, hoping against hope that I would see something of value. Or maybe a clue as to what they had found. When I was on my third pass-through, the idea hatched in my mind.

Yes, sneaking onto a fossil dig site at night wasn't the *safest* plan, but my phone could take great low-light pictures. Hell, my cell light wasn't terrible in a pinch either. I might just be able to snag some shots of whatever it was they found and fix the saturation on my laptop.

Was it stupid?

Yes.
Was it the stupidest thing I'd ever done?
Hell no.
Pop in, pop out, and get those damn fossil pictures.
Take that, Ballcap, you stingy asshole.

CHAPTER THREE

ROYAL

"Why exactly do I have to do at night again?" The sun had quietly tucked itself away when I had started my hike, and I glanced up at the stars as I walked. The crescent moon was haloed by thin clouds, the stars equally soft and beautiful.

"The small creatures most of us turned into during the asteroid impact were nocturnal," Montana explained over the phone. "All of you—Baha, Dalton and yourself—woke up at night. It's optimal since that means there likely won't be any humans around."

"Let's say I get there, and there is a shifter crawling up from the ground like a damn zombie. What am I supposed to do?" I shivered at the thought of a ghoulish form pushing up from the dirt. We weren't zombies, I knew that, but what if this one was? Hell, what if it was a zombie prehistoric thing that wanted to tear my face off?

"Do you remember when you woke up? How it felt? What you saw?"

"A little bit." I had the urge to rub at my neck. It had been forty years ago, but I remembered that night in fuzzy clips. My memory was grainy and missing pieces, but the feeling was still there.

Confusion.

Weakness.

Soul-crushing fear.

Nothing had been like I had remembered it. I had fallen asleep with the world on fire and woke up on a cold planet I didn't understand. The air was thin, the smell all wrong. My hearing was garbage, my eyesight dull, and my sense of smell was almost nonexistent.

And my body?

Compared to the might of a Regaliceratops, a human body was a crime against nature. No horns, no frills, thin skin that could tear easily with patches of hair. Did you know how jarring it was to have your genitals just out like that? Humans really had everything vital on display.

These days, I was a big fan of being human. Language, culture, cooked food, emotions beyond just eat, sleep, fuck and fight; those were some strong selling points. I could love things now. Really, actually love things and people, not just accept them for the sake of furthering the species.

But going from that limited scope from a giant animal to a small, weak creature that's self aware was rough. I wouldn't have been surprised if a couple of us didn't survive the psychological strain of it.

"I know it's scary and confusing. When I saw you, I remember thinking you looked terrifying. No offense." I smirked as Montana chuckled.

"None taken. Just remember, Royal, be patient. Be calm. They'll mirror your emotion and pick up on it faster than we're used to with humans. They'll be so hyper-aware of your body language, they'll read that you're not a threat as long as you show them that. If you do run into one, call me. I'll walk you through it."

I let out a long breath. "Alright. Did I mention that I hate this?"

"You did. But I'm confident in you, Royal. I trust you."

"Thanks, boss." I rubbed at the warmth in my chest. Montana had always been our big brother. Getting praise from him made me gooey inside. "Hopefully, I won't be calling you back tonight. Hey, how's France?"

"A little cold, but otherwise, it's nice. Be safe." He disconnected the call after that, since Montana was too badass to say goodbye.

I slipped my phone away and pushed my hands in my hoodie pockets. It was a magnificent night, all things considered. The distant chirps of crickets and faraway calls of nocturnal animals all blended together into a blissful soundtrack. Only the sounds of my crunching boots disrupted the flow. As I neared the dig site, I could see a glow of electric light blooming from just beyond the crest of the hill. I slowed my pace and kept low as I climbed over it, hiding behind the ridge as I peeked over the site.

A couple of floodlights connected to a small generator were pointed toward the fossil bed the museum had been working on. Parked near the outcrop where they had been digging was a large, boxy Hummer hauling a flatbed trailer with a tarp tossed over it. A couple of men were milling around, walking the perimeter looking at the fossil bed.

"What the fuck?" I took out my phone and tried to zoom, but I couldn't get a good look at what was going on. Fucking thieves. I caught a band of fossil thieves in the middle of the act.

My stomach twisted into knots as anger ripped through me. These sons of bitches picked the wrong site to poach. They were going to have to deal with one pissed-off, handsome dinosaur.

Before I could properly get into ass-kicking character, I heard someone start to shout. It was too far for me to see anything at first, but the moment a human form began clawing out of the dirt, my stomach dropped.

It was happening. There was another shifter. And they were surrounded by...I don't know what.

It was the worst possible scenario next to popping to life in broad daylight around a bunch of volunteers. No, I thought this might be way worse. These thieves were about to get an eyeful of something absolutely insane.

The shifter crawled from the dirt—white skin, dark hair, turning its head around to take in everything. I held my breath as they pushed themselves from the earth, their posture low and dangerous, slowly scanning the group of humans surrounding them. I could tell from the body it was male, strong, and, by the way it wasn't screaming or panicking, meant bad fucking news.

That shifter was used to not being scared.

That's really, really bad. Sharp teeth and shitty attitude bad.

Someone was approaching him, another human guy in a gray suit, who stood just at the lip of the fossil site. I could tell he was talking, but there was no way in hell I could hear what was being said. My brain was pingponging around trying to formulate a plan. A way to intervene or at least understand what the hell was going on.

But the thieves were the least of my problems.

Because that very calm shifter started to move.

I sucked in my breath through my teeth in alarm because even from this distance, I knew what was happening. The screams of alarm solidified that as the shifter's body began to twist and grow. The shouts weren't panic or confusion, but barked orders and commands. They knew what he was.

And they were ready for this.

Or at least they thought they were.

I didn't know what other shifters they had encountered, but their controlled yelling turned into shrill fear as the shifted unfolded into a walking nightmare. The hair on the back of my neck rose, my inner beast lifted its horn in alarm.

It had been millions of years since I had seen an Albertosaurus, but they were just as fucking mean and brutal as they were back then. A twenty-five-foot, pissed-off apex predator at the top of the food chain did not like being disturbed when he just woke up.

Those humans were going to get slaughtered.

I was up and running before I really knew what I was doing. The voice in my head was screaming at me to run the *opposite* direction of the fucking tyrannosaur, but my bull side was chanting to protect. Those humans didn't stand a chance, and if he gobbled a couple of them down, I didn't know what that meant for him. They'd probably gun him down like a rabid dog.

Dalton had told me before that Montana told him never to eat humans. He also mentioned that humans apparently tasted like plastic.

So there's something you know now.

But I had no idea what humans tasted like to an Albertosaurus. And we weren't going to find out today.

Running and stripping was extremely difficult. My hoodie and shirt came off easily, but getting my boots, socks, boxers, and pants off weren't nearly as graceful. I also had never shifted in mid-run before, so when I tripped and hit the dirt, I was thankful no one was watching me. My body popped and contorted, my human side falling away as my bull Regaliceratops pushed forward. My skull grew backwards, fanning out into my prized, studded frill. My brow horns pierced through my hide, as did my much bigger nose horn that rested above my beak.

My body was huge, a walking tank with enough power to crush bones when I charged at full speed. And I was hauling major ass as I heard the pissy theropod start to growl. He was too preoccupied with the scurrying humans that he didn't see me coming. I tilted my head down as I smashed into his side, using my frill to connect to his ribs instead of my horn.

I didn't want to kill him. I just wanted him away from the little bite-sized mammals he was eying. The Albertosaurus rolled across the ground, taking out a tent and ripping the caution tape around the site. I stood my ground as he slowly got to his feet, eyes dark, jaws lowered to state me down.

Oh, yes. You recognize me. You know me. I'm familiar. I'm the past roaring back to life.

Defend. Protect.

I gave him a low warning, putting myself in front of the camp of humans.

Not yours. Back down.

The smell of a predator around me was so ancient and raw, something I hadn't tasted for so long. The only big therapods in my life now were my brothers, and their scent was home and safety.

This guy made my belly boil and my heart pound. Danger. Death.

He stared at me like I was dinner.

I lowered my horns.

This dinner will put holes in you.

His body language changed suddenly. His body lowered, his head down; the fierceness in his eyes that was tinted with hunger morphed to something else.

Fear.

Submission.

For a couple brief, pride-boosting moments, I thought this big slab of teeth was scared of me. I was a bull, after all, with a big frill and knocked the piss out of him just moments prior.

But he wasn't scared of me.

He was scared of the bigger theropod behind me.

A big, angry, brutal as hell Giganotosaurus.

BLAISE

WHAT THE *HELL* WAS GOING ON?

Did I hit my head on the hike out to the site and slip into a weird coma? If what was happening was playing out in my imagination, I clearly need some therapy and to dial back the dinosaur documentaries before bed.

Because what.

The.

Actual.

Fuck.

It was already weird as hell to see a damn rogue ops camp set up around the dig site like they found some buried treasure or something, but seeing a guy exhume himself from the earth like a horror movie villain had been the icing on the cake.

But oh, no. That wasn't icing. That was just more fucking cake in the trauma dessert. We'd graduated from repressed memory pastries to sci-fi parfaits when the horror movie villain turned into a fucking tyrannosaur.

From snout to tail, the dinosaur's hide was dark with bands of color fading in around his thighs. His neck was almost silvery gray, the tips of his claws obsidian and sharp. The only blast of color on him was around the eyes where a proud and distinctive ridge formed around them. The sharp shade of red stood out among all the monochrome.

Let's pause a second to discuss how backwards my priorities are, by the way. The man crawls from the dirt and explodes into a prehistoric fever dream, and instead of running in terror or calling the police, *I zoom in with my camera to try and figure out what species he is.*

Ok, Blaise. This is why you're going to be the first to die in an apocalypse. Oh, big scary monster? Let me look at how many fucking fingers it has.

It had two. Therefore, it's a tyrannosaur. Good job, me. Gold star.

And I wasn't done. Yeah, there's more "what the fuck is wrong with you, Blaise" ammo here.

So the now-identified tyrannosaur was eying these goons in white scrubs like they were appetizers, and I saw a flash of color racing towards the site from the hill. At first, I wasn't sure what the hell I was seeing, but then the loud color palette pulled forward a memory from a booze-fueled night of depravity.

I knew that hoodie. That ugly as hell, 90's arcade floor with little neon dinosaurs attached to the hot hookup from the club. The same hot hookup I had let do deliciously sinful things to me in a dark corner of a gay bar. Hottie was bolting towards the camp at full speed, like he just couldn't wait to get gobbled up by the massive dinosaur looming over it.

I stared in complete shock and disbelief, only registering after his shirt went flying that the man was stripping while he ran.

And you know what I did?

Did I yell for him to stop or try to do anything to help him? Oh, no.

I zoomed in on him to see what was happening. And by what was happening, I mean his ass.

I winced as he got one boot off and fell to the ground, not even bothering to dust himself off as he scrambled back to his feet again. Socks, pants, and boxers went flying, and I got the best view of his tight backside before his body started to...morph.

Maybe it's because I spent my youth devouring books about shapeshifters or my love for monster movies, but I wasn't as horrified as I probably should have been. I didn't recoil in fear, scream like a banshee, or faint like a Southern belle. I marveled at the offense of nature like one would admire a sunrise.

Just like with the guy in the dirt, Hottie started to twist and bulge, his skin stretching over bones and muscles that grew outward in impossible shapes. His head elongated and widened, his body ballooned up and out, hunching until he was on all fours. A tail sprouted from his spine, his ebony skin changing into a deep red, almost rusty orange color.

His misshapen skull unfolded into a frill, topped with flat, plate-like horns along the ridge. Two small brow horns appeared over his eyes, and a bigger one topped his nose like a rhino's horn. I recognized what he was immediately.

He was a fucking Regaliceratops.

There was a tiny piece of my brain that whispered, "You let a hot, shapeshifting dinosaur impregnate your throat. You have to deal with this."

Lots to unpack there.

Watching a full-grown ceratopsian bulldoze into a massive tyrannosaur was simultaneously the coolest and most stressful thing I had ever witnessed. It was like watching a childhood fantasy come to life, but with the very real sense of death that came with being an adult. Yes, it was badass, but I also knew the level of destruction that was possible. Hottie-Tops sent the theropod rolling, his head lowered as he dared the bastard to get back on his feet.

You know that floating feeling you get when you're having a really vivid dream? Like when you're able to push off the ground and take flight, or when you find yourself meandering down a river of orange soda with your high school crush? (That's normal, right?)

I had that floating sensation as I moved, my legs on autopilot before my brain could really catch up. Seeing something so unbelievably insane, like a bunch of living, breathing, *fighting* dinosaurs, was enough to fry any sane or logical connections in my brain. Some of those apparently were also linked to self-preservation because I had decided I needed to get closer.

Now, I wasn't an overly brave man, but I also took calculated risks. It was a risk to spend what I had to limp my car to Alberta. It was a risk to quit my shitty job to go see more of the world. It was a risk to apply glitter eyeshadow with regular primer instead of the glitter-specific stuff.

So sneaking closer to a dinosaur fight was on brand for me.

I threw myself onto the ground and army-crawled closer once I felt like I was at a safe distance, unlocking my phone and swiping until I got to the livestream option. My hands were shaking, and the lens dropped in and out of focus as it tried to lock on the swift movement of the creatures.

"I don't know what I'm seeing," I admitted once the stream started. "But if I'm going crazy, you're all coming with me."

Hottie-Tops and angry tyrannosaur were still squaring off, horns slashing as jaws snapped. Dust was flying; shadows played against the halo of dirt around the dueling dinosaurs. They had been so focused on each other that they missed the bigger monster looming in the darkness. I didn't know where the other dinosaur came from. It seemed to materialize from nothing right behind Hottie-Tops like a prehistoric boogieman. My breath caught in my chest, my heart hammering as the biggest animal I had ever seen stepped into the floodlights.

I grew up a dinosaur kid. I knew dinosaurs like the back of my hand.

There was no mistaking a Giganotosaurus. Big as a T.rex, but with a narrow snout and defined ridges over its brows. The damn thing looked like something that crawled out of hell, with a dark hide and long, deadly teeth. The tension in my chest made breathing impossible, each sharp inhale a vice around my lungs.

It was pointless to try, but I screamed for Hottie-Tops to look out. Watching a huge therapod bite down into Hottie-Top's back made me sick to my stomach. I covered my eyes like a coward, terrified of watching him getting killed in front of me. The bellowing howl of pain that ripped from Hottie-Top was like a punch in the gut. The helplessness I felt made me shrink, and I felt about as useful as a mouse in the middle of a dinosaur fight.

I knew in my gut that the moment I slipped my fingers away from my eyes, I'd see Hottie-Tops torn to pieces. I had seen plenty of artists' drawings of what it may have looked like to watch a massive meat-eater tearing a leg off of a leaf-eater. We all saw *Land Before Time.* Hottie-Tops would be Littlefoot's mom, and I would probably never recover.

As I peeked around my fingers to accept my future trauma, I was surprised to see that Hottie-Top hadn't been turned into dinner. He was backed away, bloody and hurt, with his horns lowered. Had the Giga let him go? The massive, deadly bastard in question had his nose to the air. The sound of him sniffing was like hearing a whale take a breath from the water's surface. His narrow snout of death lowered slowly.

And he looked at *me.*

He could smell me. Of *course* he could smell me. I was a tiny appetizer who had crawled close enough to see his damn pupils flexing my direction. God, I wished in that moment that

Jurassic Park had been right about the motion thing with these big ones. I had also wished that I wasn't in a brightly colored shirt with a scarf on.

"Fuck."

A terrifying sound rumbled from the beast, a weirdly crocodilian bellow mixed with a hiss that made my insides turn into liquid. My limbs were about as useful as overcooked noodles as I tried to get up and run, the fear racing through me numbing all of my sensations.

I was going to die.

I was going to get *eaten alive* by a dinosaur. On camera.

The ground slid under me as I got to my feet, dust and rocks rolling under my feet as I stood and hauled ass. It felt like I was running underwater, going too slow for the building-sized wall of death walking towards me. While he strolled, I pushed my legs to their limit, racing faster than I had ever moved. But it was like watching an ant run from a shoe. No matter how fast I went, it wasn't going to save me.

Nothing was going to save me.

I whipped my head over my shoulder to see how much time I had left before I was snatched off the earth in knife-lined jaws, when a crimson badass slammed into the thigh of the monster chasing me. Hottie-Top's nose horn punctured through the hide and muscle, knocking the Giga sideways with a painful roar. The other tyrannosaur who had been fighting with Hottie-Tops earlier turned tail and fled, leaving the bleeding Giga on the ground.

Hottie-Tops did the same, racing away while the biggest thing with sharp teeth was down. His shape began to shrink as he galloped, the morph going in reverse from giant to human sized. A naked, bloody, panting man rushed to my side and grabbed my arm, hauling me faster towards the horizon.

We scrambled away, running for what felt like a lifetime

before I finally dared to look over my shoulder. The Giganotosaurus was limping away from us in the direction of the tyrannosaur.

"He's not following us," I panted, slowing to a trot before leaning over with my palms on my knees. It burned to breathe as hard as I was, and there had been a couple close calls with puking my guts out.

Hottie-Tops was breathing hard as well, but not nearly as badly as I was. His back was raw and bloody, but he covered it with his discarded hoodie that we had run close to. As he got dressed, I saw the pain ripple over his features with each movement.

"We should get you to a hospital," I managed between gulping down air. "And maybe call the FBI or something."

"Neither of those." His fingers shook as he tried to fish his phone from his pants. When he finally did, it fell to the ground, and he hissed a string of curses.

"How did I know," I paused to catch more of my breath, "that you were going to say that?"

"I need to get back to my hotel." He tried to bend down to get his phone and hissed through his teeth. I straightened myself from where I was hunched over trying not to pass out and gathered his phone for him. I took his hand and pressed the phone into his palm.

"Look. I have a first-aid kit at my place. At least come let me clean you up. Okay? You're like a human chew toy right now."

Was "human" the right word?

He nodded. "I guess you have a lot of questions."

"Uh, yeah." I exhaled. "Just a couple."

CHAPTER FOUR

ROYAL

"Stop being such a baby."

The cute twink waited until I relaxed my back after jerking away from the icy sting. I sat with my chest pressed against the back of a chair, my punctured back facing him as he cleaned up the wounds. It felt like I had been stabbed with a dozen steak knives, each going just deep enough to send a spiderweb of pain across my back.

"Are they deep?" I glanced over my shoulder as he worked, his brows furrowed as he concentrated. His short, auburn curly hair spiraled over his brow, his fair skin flushed from our sprinting earlier. The very tips of his curls were pale green from long-faded dye, which made his hazel eyes seem mossy. His touch of color and slight frame had been what urged me to buy him a drink last night.

Among other things.

"Not as deep as I thought they would be. I don't think you need stitches, but we'll have to keep these cleaned off. Hold still!"

"It hurts!" I snapped. "You try dealing with getting your back gnawed on, man. It burns like a bitch."

"I'll pass, thanks." He blew out some air from his nose and tried to steady my shoulder as he flushed each of the bite marks. The rush of icy pain that hit each time he treated one made me tense and jerk, but I tried like hell to hold still. When he was finally putting bandages over them, the pain had eased into a more manageable, dull ache.

"Okay, that'll do for now." He stood and handed me a glass of water. "Are you still shaking?"

I shook my head, sipping the water. "No. Thanks." I lifted my eyes as he dragged his chair over in front of me, spun it around to mirror how I was straddling mine, and then sat down facing me. He crossed his arms over the back of the old office chair and rested his chin on them, burrowing his hazel eyes into mine.

The last little bit of eyeliner he was wearing earlier in the day was almost completely faded. A washed-out smudge of blue disappearing against his dark lashes.

He held out his hand to me. "I'm Blaise, by the way. Blaise Fite."

I took his hand and squeezed. "Royal."

A snort of laughter escaped him, and he narrowed his eyes. "That's your real name?" When I nodded, he huffed again. "Fitting. So. Royal." He made a flourish with his hand towards me. "Care to tell me what the fuck happened tonight?"

I blinked, sipping my water. "Would you buy that I have amnesia?"

"No."

"What if I told you I was bitten by a radioactive fossil, and now I fight crime as Dino-Man?"

"You *have* to tell me what the hell is going on, Royal. I just watched you turn into a Regaliceratops like you're a fucking Animorph." When I raised my eyebrows in surprise that he knew my species, he gave me the most scathing look. "Oh, you don't get to look at me like *I'm* the crazy one for knowing what a Regaliceratops is, honey."

"*Honey?*" I snorted. "You are sassy when you're flustered."

Blaise's slow inhale through his nose was like listening to a fuse being lit. "Royal, I swear to God."

"Okay, easy. Easy." I rubbed a hand down my face. It wasn't like I could dance around it forever. My cover was blown. Hell, not just mine. RELIC's was. All of ours was. Blaise, a human, saw me shift. He saw the other shifter and...whoever the hell that Giganotosaurus was. He witnessed it all.

Montana was going to be so pissed.

For a second, I thought about making up some huge lie about being a government experiment, or maybe that we were fallen gods, mutants, aliens—something about as ridiculous as the truth. Maybe. But the way Blaise's eyes were laser-focused on my face, I had a sneaking suspicion he was waiting for me to pull some bullshit.

Even though this human with faded green hair was staring me down like *he* was the bull in the herd, I did owe him for helping me. I don't know many people who'd run into a dinosaur fight like he had done. He had guts.

"Okay. This is going to sound insane, but I'm not lying to you," I began slowly, watching Blaise's eyes squint as he analyzed my words. He was like a human lie detector.

"Uh-huh," he supplied slowly. "Go on."

"I can't speak for the other two you saw today, but I assume they're the same as me. I've been around for, hell, as long as life has been on this planet. From the tiniest little microorganisms to multi-celled dynamos like what you see before you. I used to move from form to form, adapting into whatever I needed to in order to survive. I don't know how, and I don't know why." I paused to let his lie-detector eyes scan me, one eyebrow raising as he nodded for me to continue.

"About sixty-five million years and some change back, a big-ass space rock slapped the planet into another mass extinction. Probably the second-least-favorite one after the Permian, but that's only because I really liked being an Edaphosaurus."

Blaise wrinkled his nose. "Seriously?"

"Do you have something to say about Edaphosaurus?" Yeah, I was a big, lumbering synapsid in my youth. Who the hell wasn't? Baha wasn't the only one who got to be the big baddie with the sail.

At least I wasn't a proud Eyrops like Dalton. Who the fuck was proud of being a Eyrops? My brother had some issues.

"Not a Dimetrodon?"

"I'm a vegetarian."

Blaise raised his palms and shook his head. "Excuse the shit out of me. Go on."

"That's what I thought." I sniffed. "Anyway, sixty-five whatever million years ago, asteroid hits, and I shift into the smallest thing I could and burrow down into the dirt to escape the chaos. When I wake up, it's the 1980s, I'm a human, and my ability to move forms is out of whack. Now I'm either this handsome gent or my dapper Ornithischian form."

"Why the change?" Blaise asked, shrugging his shoulders up as he asked the question. "What about the asteroid striking the earth would change your abilities?"

"I have no clue." A long sigh escaped as I answered. "I wish I did. Do you believe me so far?"

"You don't seem like you're lying, but I also have no way of verifying anything you're saying other than the fact that I saw you defy the laws of nature like forty-five minutes ago. So, I mean...sure? I guess?"

It was my turn to eye him suspiciously. "You're handling all this remarkably well."

"Oh, I'm going to have a full mental breakdown later, probably at a really inopportune time," Blaise assured me. "So who the fuck were those tyrannosaurs? Old boyfriends?"

I snorted a laugh. "I don't date meat-eaters."

"So, *so* many jokes." He practically giggled himself out of the chair, then inhaled and composed himself. "But seriously. What the hell was that about?"

"The guy who you saw crawling out of the dirt? He just woke up. I was hoping to take him in and help get him on his feet. When we wake up after *the Epoch Nap*, we don't know what the hell is going on. It's like going to bed, and the next morning you're on Mars, and you've taken the form of a squid, and other squids are demanding answers to why you're there, but you don't speak squid and can now understand your own mortality."

Blaise's eyebrows climbed. "That's fucking intense and...weirdly specific. Wait, are you saying you think humans are like squids?"

"Basically."

"Ouch."

I clicked my tongue. "How do you think I feel?"

Blaise let out a breath through his lips and ran his fingers through his curls. His eyes finally switched from scanning mode to bewilderment as he let everything sink in.

"Why did that Giganotosaurus attack you? Was he also a new shifter?"

"No, he couldn't be. Giganotosaurus are from Argentina, not Canada. I have no clue who that was, why he was there, or why the asshole attacked me." I winced as my standing tugged at my wounds. "But I need to make a call."

"Who are you going to call?"

"Ghostbusters." I scooped up my hoodie and grabbed my phone from where I placed it.

"Wow, you really are from the eighties, Grandpa," he deadpanned, and I gasped with mock offense.

"We prefer to be called silver foxes, you fucking rugrat." I wiggled my phone. "I'm calling my team. And—" I stopped him before he could ask. "I'll tell you about them later. One massive infodump at a time, shall we? I can't destroy all of our secrets in one sitting because that's more of a second date kind of thing."

"If this is a date, lose my number. This shit," he waved a finger in a big circle, to encompass the entire clusterfuck of a night, "is specifically my 'Don'ts' on Grindr."

"Not into life-or-death stakes with Kaiju-style dinosaur fights while learning the existence of a prehistoric life that takes different forms on the first date? How boring."

Blaise leaned forward with his chest pressing into the back of the chair, his hazel eyes narrowed into little blades of glass. "No, I'm just into meat-eaters."

"So am I."

"Ah-ha. Well played." Blaise rolled his eyes, and his cheeks flushed. "Go make your call. I have to go throw up and pass out."

I went out into the brisk evening air, standing on the stairs leading up to the small apartment. My nerves were frayed from the events of the day, and I had no damn clue how I was going to explain this all to Montana.

Breaking this kind of thing is more of a morning thing, right? I should wait for tomorrow.

Exhaling, I dialed his number. I had no clue what time it was in France, but I knew he'd answer no matter what. Damn the reliable asshole.

"Status." His voice was a little gravelly from sleep, but he still sounded alert.

"Hey, boss." I rubbed at my neck. "I have some news. You might wanna grab a fresh cup of coffee."

"Did you find something?" I could hear the bed creak as he moved, the dull flick of a light switch soon after.

"Sort of," I hedged, before I slowly began explaining the entire night. Describing the thieves, the shifter waking up from the dirt and the surprise, cheap shot Giganotosaurus made me feel like I had dreamed the entire thing. After laying out the events, I took a long breath and rubbed my temple, exhaustion starting to settle bone-deep.

There was silence on the other end of the line. I pulled back to check the connection.

"Montana?"

"I'm here," he said in a low tone. "I'm just trying to process what you told me. Are you alright? How bad are your injuries?"

"My back feels like a chew toy, but I'm okay. Do you know who that asshole Giganotosaurus was? An old friend of yours from before we met?"

"No." He sighed deeply. "No, I don't. What happened to the Albertosaurus?"

"I dunno. Last I saw, he was taking off when I was. The fucker could only follow one of us, so he went for him."

"Fuck." Our leader was never one to get flustered, but I could hear the frustration in his voice.

"What's the plan now? What do you want me to do?"

"Lie low. Get some rest. If you can, see what information you can find out tomorrow. I need to try and get a flight out of here."

I leaned back against the door and hissed, forgetting about my back. "Have you gone out to your site yet?"

"Not yet. That was my plan for tonight."

"Boss, go visit your site. I don't want you to miss out on something important. I can do some recon while you're working."

"Royal, I don't want you going back out there alone."

"They've gotta be long gone by now, right? There's no way in hell they'd stick around if they could help it."

"We don't know their plan, and we have no info on them. There's no telling what will be waiting out there now."

I glanced back towards the apartment door. Technically, I wasn't alone. Blaise wasn't RELIC, but he was another set of eyes.

"I'll be careful. Trust me, I don't plan on making myself known out there again. But I can snoop safely."

"Keep me updated."

"Likewise."

I glanced down at the phone as Montana disconnected. Going back out to that site was the last thing I wanted to do, but I couldn't hide here and do nothing. Tomorrow, I could go back and at least snag some pictures, or maybe try and find a way into their network. Even a high-tech, creepy base was going to have some holes in their cyber security. If I could wiggle in through any faulty backdoor, maybe I could get some idea of who the hell they were.

Back inside the apartment, I found Blaise passed out on the only bed. It looked like he crashed while checking his phone, the device still in his fingers even though he was sprawled across the mattress.

The fact that the only other person who knew what happened that night was the same random hookup I met the previous night was some lottery-winning odds. One night, he was swallowing down my dick; the next, we were trying to outrun a pissed-off theropod who was ready to slaughter us both. I didn't know this guy at all, other than he was hot and had a mouth I quite enjoyed and wasn't afraid to get up close and personal to a dinosaur fight.

Could be worse. He could be a flat earther or something.

Oh God. What if he was?

I shivered at the thought as I snagged one of the pillows from the bed and made my way to the couch. I would tackle the riddle of the mystery shifter, the lost tyrannosaur, and the hopefully not insane danger twink tomorrow.

Tonight, I was getting some well-earned sleep.

CHAPTER FIVE

BLAISE

Apparently, adrenaline-crash sleep is my jam.

I could have gone without the violent heaving and shakes beforehand, but breakdowns were what they were. Dealing with everything I had seen, almost dying, and then learning about dinosaur shape shifters tended to do a number on your psyche. And, in my case, stomach.

I slept harder than I ever had in my life. I probably would have slept all day if my phone hadn't started vibrating every other second in my hand. In an autopilot haze, I flicked the screen open to see what the hell was going on. The staggering amount of notifications on my very unpopular account woke me right up.

My feed was blowing *up*.

The video from last night had gone completely viral, shared through channels with way higher viewer counts than my own. My brush with death by way of being prehistoric meal was being praised as one of the best fan-made horror trailers ever.

I mean, I'd take it. Expecting people to believe the insanity of last night was real would be ridiculous, even if Royal had scars to prove it. The excitement of seeing the thread being shared as far out as some of the key animators on the very popular superhero movies (you know the ones) made my heart race.

This might be what I needed to get my foot in the door as an influencer. I knew that sounded trivial and maybe even ludicrous, but getting noticed in an ocean of handles was nearly impossible. And if I could make a living traveling to far-flung fossil sites talking about paleontology, I would be living my dream.

Having a viral video was a step towards that dream.

I barely registered that Royal had sat up on the couch, groaning in discomfort as he rotated his shoulder.

I had almost forgotten that my shapeshifting hookup was still here. That's how excited about this virtual video I was.

"Morning." I turned my phone off, rolling over to look at him. "How's your back?"

"Sore. Stiff." He rubbed his hand down his face and cracked one eye open to glance at me. "You don't have coffee here, do you?"

"No, but Black Mountain is just up the road. They sell breakfast and coffee there." I watched him stand and stretch, a small peek of rich umber skin flashing under his ugly sweater for just a moment.

"Sounds good. I'm starving." He disappeared into the bathroom for a while, just long enough to finally peel myself from the bed and pull my shoes on. I kept wanting to go through more of my messages and tags, but I also was very preoccupied with the knowledge that dinosaur shifters existed beyond *Jurassic Park* fanfiction and epic sci-fi novels.

I decided to wait until Royal had some coffee before starting with another round of questions.

Black Mountain coffee was a modern cafe in the heart of Drumheller. Inside this little roaster-y oasis, sleepy sunlight painted their counters in an amber glow. The t-shirts on the walls showing their logo of sharp mountains next to a roaring T.rex was an ode to the whole town's aesthetic.

I had snagged a bite to eat there the previous day, still nursing a bad hangover from the club. Nothing cured the post-licentious-night grogginess like pastries and iced coffee. I challenge you to find something that the duo doesn't cure.

I ordered the tried and true sweet, flaky delight and cold brew while Royal ordered two vegetarian breakfast sandwiches and a giant cup of coffee, with an ungodly amount of sugar in it.

"Good lord," I finally said when he opened another packet and stirred it in. "How are you that jacked if you eat that much sugar?"

One of his meaty shoulders rose in a sleepy shrug. "Ceratopsians have kickass metabolisms."

"Huh." I took a heavenly bite from my pastry and wiped some chocolate from my lips. The conversation died as we ate, both of us focused on draining our coffee and devouring the food in front of us. Once it was finished, the quiet stretched from the polite absence of noise to deafening silence.

"So. Um." Royal cleared his throat. "I guess we should address that we've met prior to last night."

Ah, yes. *The Talk.*

There was no way we could avoid it. One didn't typically run into your wild, one-night stand in a life-or-death event the next day unless you were living in a spy novel or something. Maybe Royal was a dino-spy, but I definitely wasn't a Bond Girl.

But Daniel Craig could love me and leave me any day.

"You mean when I performed fellatio on you in a dimly lit gay bar?" I asked around my straw.

Royal coughed a laugh. "Yeah. That."

The familiar churn of nerves in my stomach almost made my breakfast revisit the table. I was very familiar with the "it was just a one-time thing" from my previous fuck buddies and former friends with benefits. It seemed as though I was a great time to be had, exactly one time. Beyond that, I was weird, annoying, clingy, or—and this was my favorite—confusing. Yeah, that's a fun confidence booster. All these little gems were the sparkle in my shitty personality and the shine in my emotional distance crown.

"What's there to talk about?" I mirrored his previous lazy, one-shoulder shrug. "It was fun, but that's old news. We don't need to make things complicated."

I stabbed at the bottom of my plastic cup with my straw, flicking my phone screen so I didn't have to watch the relief wash over his face.

"Oh. Sure." He crumpled up his napkin and tossed it onto his plate. "I guess that's probably best."

"Yep." I placed my chin in my hand and glanced up at him. "So, what's the plan today, Brain? We taking over the world?"

"Not so much. I need to get back out to the site to see if I can get any clues to who these fuckers are."

"You want to go back out there?" My eyebrow popped up. "Do you have a grenade launcher handy in case King Asshole comes back?"

"I doubt they're still out there, but I don't plan on being seen if they are. I'm hoping they were stupid enough to leave something behind or at least some tracks for us to follow."

"Us?" I smirked. "Am I invited?"

"Two pairs of eyes are better. Maybe you'll spot something I don't. If you're up for it, anyway."

"I'm up for finding out more about the dinosaur part, not so much being eaten."

"Same." He lifted his chin towards my empty plate. "You done? I want to get moving."

"Lead the way, sugar-saurus."

Early spring mornings in Canada were still chilly. Royal seemed content in his loud sweater that looked a little rough from last night, but I was layered up and wrapped my cute scarf around my chin. Being born here didn't mean I liked the cold or handled it well. I craved the summer each year, and each year, it seemed to drag its feet more and more. Hiking back out to the site was uncomfortable, but not awful. It also gave me time to ask a cute dinosaur more questions.

"So." I sipped my coffee. "You have a team? Are they Regaliceratops too? Are you all a herd of big, badass horned bounty hunters or something?"

"Sadly, I'm the only ceratopsian in a whole mess of theropods."

I blinked at him. "Your team is all theropods? How the hell does that work? Don't they want to eat you?"

Royal smiled. The warmth in his expression stung my jealousy nerve. "Nah. They're like my brothers, really. Montana found us. He's been around the longest. He scooped us up when we were waking up, brought us home, and helped guide us through understanding what had happened. He taught us English, kept us safe, educated us about the world, and kept us out of trouble. Now we help track down stolen fossils and get them into the hands of museums and universities or get them sent back to their native countries."

"You steal back stolen fossils?" I cut my eyes towards him. "And not like...fight crime?"

"How the fuck would we fight crime and not get seen?" He furrowed his brow at me, laughter coloring his words. "No, man. We rescue fossils and help the world understand its past. We want humans to know about us, our legacy, and where they came from."

"And rescue other shifters?" I supplied. "Or is that a new thing?"

Royal huffed, annoyance sharpening his tone. "It's new for me. I'm not the guy that usually gets sent on these missions."

"What do you mean? Why wouldn't you be?"

"Are you too young to know the Ninja Turtles?"

"Oh my God, Royal." I scoffed, offended. "I'm twenty-six."

"So, no?"

I tried to shove him playfully, but it was like trying to jokingly nudge a boulder. So it was a little awkward, and he laughed at me.

"I fucking know the Ninja Turtles, asshole."

"I'm Donatello. My buddy Dalton is Mikey, Baha is Raph, Montana is Leo, and Yu is Splinter if Splinter was a little more weird and eccentric. And kinda into poison and fashion. That's my family."

"Okay, your family sounds terrifying. Those personalities on theropods is terrifying, Royal."

"I'm not arguing with you," he said around a laugh. "But you see why I'm not pleased to be thrown into this shit. This isn't a Donny fight. I need my technology and to not be chomped at."

"Yeah, but Donny is also a trained fighter, and you're a dinosaur. You'll be fine," I argued.

"Strong disagree, B."

"Whatever you say, Donny."

The rest of the hike Royal told me about his brothers and some of the missions they had gone on. Dalton had found his boyfriend during his last heist, escaping the cartel and rescuing an oviraptor egg. I knew the one he was talking about. I had been following the thief from the American Museum of Natural History a couple months back.

Baha had fallen in love with a former fossil thief and nearly died on a cruise ship that was hosting a fossil auction off the coast of Portugal. He claimed that their score was the original holotype Spinosaurus fossils that were supposed to have been destroyed in World War II.

I had my doubts, but I kept that to myself.

Having a family made up of a Utahraptor, Spinosaurus, Yutyrannus and T.rex was a hell of a mix. Royal really was the only veggie-saurus in a house of deadly predators.

I doubted from how massive he was that he let any of those guys push him around. I had seen him as Regaliceratops, and he was just as impressive. He drove a horn through a Giganotosaurus like it was made of paper.

He was definitely stronger than he thought.

Me on the other hand, I was totally ill-equipped to deal with this fight. But when had that ever slowed me down?

"Hey, so what are your thoughts on the shape of the earth?" Royal asked, and I glanced at him, bewildered.

"What?" I shielded my eyes from the sun as I peered over the horizon. We had gotten close enough to the fossil site to see activity buzzing around it. Instead of runaway theropods and floodlights, the familiar matching colors of the museum's volunteer team dotted the bone bed. "Yep, you were right. King Asshole and Sleeping Beauty are gone."

"Fuck," Royal sighed. "I figured they would be. Hopefully, the volunteers didn't step all over anything they may have left behind."

I followed as he continued towards the site. "Yeah, well, unless you're part of their team, they're not going to let you anywhere near the site. Trust me."

"You've been out here before?" Royal glanced my way, and I rolled my eyes.

"Oh, yeah. Before the fuckery of last night, I tried to come out here to get some interviews and pictures. See the old dude in the ballcap? He basically told me to scram since I wasn't a volunteer. Said I'd *step all over* the fossils." I stage-whispered, "I think he was jealous of my scarf and big gay dinosaur pin."

"I'm jealous of your scarf and big gay dinosaur pin," Royal added. "But leave the old white guy to me."

I huffed and hung back a bit as Old Ballcap's eagle vision landed on us. The closer we came to the site, the more pinched his face seemed to get. His eyes definitely lingered on me long enough to know he wasn't happy to see me again, and his skepticism towards Royal was boldly apparent.

"Can I help you gentlemen? This is a volunteer-only site from the Tyrell Museum," Ballcap said, his eyes landing on me before moving back to Royal.

"I'm aware. I'm Augustus Kingston with the Field Museum in Chicago," Royal explained with a smile, holding his hand out. Old Ballcap's eyes went wide, and he took Royal's hand enthusiastically.

"Oh, of course! Brandon told me you reached out to him earlier in the week about coming by. I can show you around the site and let you know what we've been uncovering."

"Sounds great. Blaise, could you grab some pictures of us for the social media account?" Royal waved me forward and gave Ballcap another charming smile. "Amazing what social media can do for science communication, right? Blaise here is an intern with us. He mentioned he tried coming out here yesterday, but I think there was a miscommunication of some kind?"

Oh, the look on Old Ballcap's face when he realized he done fucked up. I had to bite my cheek to keep from grinning like an idiot as he tripped over himself in apologizing.

Augustus Kingston. Jesus Christ. Royal was ridiculous.

"Don't forget to get pictures all around the site, B," Royal instructed with a wink as he kept Ballcap busy, asking about the site, volunteers, weather, whatever he could. I didn't waste time as I started carefully scanning for anything of note that might help us track down whoever was here last night.

The tire tracks from the Hummer were mixed with the truck the volunteers had brought in. I could make out where the big toe claws from the theropods dug into the dirt, racing away from the site and curving to the east. Where the hell they went after that was a mystery, as the prints died away after a couple yards, ending with faded tire tracks before going cold.

I definitely didn't see any obvious places one could stash a massive dinosaur, let alone two of them.

When I meandered back to the site, I decided to finally get a look at where the shifter had climbed out of last night. Along a rough outcrop, volunteers had dug into the earth to uncover a large, black, fossilized ribcage still stuck into dark-colored rock. I made a very unprofessional squeak of joy as I eased my way over to the fossil to take a better look.

"It's so pretty!" I said as I kneeled down to take pictures of the onyx bone. One of the volunteers grinned from under her sunhat, scraping away at the dirt still covering the rest of the skeleton.

"We're pretty sure it's a hadrosaur. Isn't it so cool to see it uncovered? We've been working on it for months."

"It's *gorgeous.* How long have you been volunteering?" I glanced over to smile at her as she worked. It was easy to tell she knew her way around a trowel, and the sun-kissed shade of her cheeks spoke to her dedication. Her volunteer shirt was clean but stained from months of dirt and sweat ingrained in the fibers, and her jeans were worn thin from kneeling in the rocks.

"About six years now. This is the best find I've been part of, but that's just because I like Hadrosaurus. Everyone always cheers for the big meat-eaters, but these sweet animals were just as important."

"I'm a pretty big fan of ceratopsians, myself," I couldn't help but say that with a grin, and it was almost impossible not to look towards Royal. I thought after all this madness I was always going to have at least a little bit of a fondness for the horned dinosaurs.

I might have still had a bit of a crush on the Regaliceratops that met me in that club the other night. Even if I knew we weren't going down that road again. Maybe I always would. It's a flaw of mine, getting loved on by a hunky dinosaur who would then leave me a little heartbroken.

I think I might put that on my tombstone, actually.

"It never gets old, uncovering something like this," she sighed wistfully. "But every now and then you get some punk kids who vandalize it."

"Vandalize the fossil?" I looked up from my phone after snapping a couple more pictures. "What do you mean?"

She pushed to her feet and pointed with her trowel down to the furthest rib. "There. Someone came last night and took a chunk out of the rib here."

I crawled over to peer at what she was talking about. Sure enough, there was a rectangle the size of my palm carved into the last rib barely poking out of the rock.

"Ew." I snarled at the ugly blemish, taking a picture of it. It was cut very precisely, a perfect shape etched directly out of the bone. "Why would they do this?"

"Who knows. Probably just to say they have a fossil or a piece of one. It's sad, isn't it? People can be so selfish."

"Amen." I grabbed a couple more shots of it before I turned to her. "Do you want to be interviewed about the site? You can share all of your knowledge about the dinosaur fossils here to the world." I wiggled my phone.

"Oh, I look terrible." She laughed, trying to push more of her wispy curls back under her hat.

"You look darling. Plus, if you're not a little dirty, you can't be on my social media," I added with a wink, and she laughed.

CHAPTER SIX

ROYAL

The old guy Blaise was having trouble with, Jeff, wasn't particularly helpful.

He couldn't remember any other visitors coming by the site, didn't recall seeing anything strange, and was more interested in trying to name-drop paleontologists he knew than actually answering my questions. By the time we were wrapping up, I had a headache and wanted a drink.

Blaise bounced over like he had knocked back a couple of espresso shots, all smiles and excitement.

"I got so many good shots. And Ashley did a *great* interview about volunteering out here. Did you know she actually was one of the volunteers who helped do the reconstruction of the Regaliceratops skull for the museum?"

"No shit?" I smiled at that. "That's kinda badass."

"Where do you want me to stand for my interview?" Jeff fixed his faded ballcap. "I've been heading the volunteer sites for years. You know, I actually was just talking with Phil Currie the other day—"

"Oh, sorry," Blaise said with poisonous sincerity, "I got all the interviews I needed. Ashley answered all of my questions just fine." His sharp smile was tight. The full grin only truly returned when he glanced down at his phone. "Oooh! Riley Black just shared it. Hell yes!"

"Ready to go?" I smirked as Blaise nodded, not quite looking up from his screen.

"All set, Mr Kingston. I got some shots I think you'll be very interested in."

I waited until we were far enough away to snicker, bumping Blaise with my elbow.

"You really pissed him off."

"Good, fuck that guy. I don't care about interviewing him. I wanted to interview the normal people who get their hands dirty because they love it. Ashley is a retired science teacher who does this on the weekends because she loves history. That is the kind of people we can relate to. Not 'I was having lunch with Phil Currie' over there. Prick. Anyway," he swiped at his screen before handing me his phone, "I couldn't find much on the tracks, except that it looks like they were eastbound. But look at the fossil there. They said they think some kids came and did that."

Displayed on the screen was a picture of the bones the volunteers were working on. Carved out of the rib was a rectangle about five inches long and three inches deep, done with expert precision.

"This was a professional," I spat. "Definitely not some kids."

"Like maybe the guys from last night?" Blaise shielded his eyes as he looked up at me.

"That's my guess." I passed his phone back to him. "There was no way they were going to be able to steal a huge fossil still stuck in the rock, so they took a piece they could sell off for a quick buck."

"God, that's so shitty. But why would a shifter like you be part of a group that butchers fossils?"

"Not all of us feel the same connection to fossils and history that we do. Hell, Baha's boyfriend was a former thief. To him, they were just rocks." I took a long breath and exhaled my frustration. "Still rubs me the wrong way, though. And now I'm even more worried about the new shifter. Who the hell knows what they're going to do with him if they don't give a shit about our legacy?"

Blaise shivered and checked his phone as it lit up with activity.

"Is the interview taking off that well?" I asked, glancing at his screen.

"Yeah, a little, but it's nothing compared to the stream from last night."

That stopped me in my tracks. "The what?"

Blaise paused and blinked. "Uh...shit."

"Blaise." I rubbed a hand down my face. "Don't tell me you recorded last night and posted it on social media."

"Of fucking course I streamed it!" Blaise shrilled. "Dinosaurs were walking around! You *wouldn't* stream that?"

"Jesus, Blaise!" I felt the blood drain from my face when I saw the amount of re-posts and comments. "No one is supposed to know about us!"

"Well do a better job about not Godzilla-fighting out in public then! Don't yell at me!"

Oh my God. There was no way to contain it now. It was out. It was everywhere. I could tear the original video down, but tracking down the copies would be impossible at this point. Maybe a virus? Just the thought of trying to construct that made me feel sick.

I couldn't blame Blaise. He didn't know. The blowback from Montana would be rough...if I decided to tell him about it. Our fearless leader tended to stress out when things were out of his control. And this was absolutely out of our control now.

"What are they saying about it?" I didn't want to know, but I had to ask.

"Everyone thinks it's fake, obviously. I'm getting some exposure, but by animators asking what program I used. And a couple nerds saying my Albertosaurus didn't look realistic."

That was kinda funny, and I failed at hiding my laugh behind a cough. Small victories. I'd probably need to try and get it hacked up or buried sooner than later, though.

"What are they saying about me?"

Blaise cut his eyes towards me. "I thought you were a dirty little secret?"

"Nothing little about me."

"Oh-ho." Blaise teased, flicking the screen before clearing his throat. "I believe 'thicc' has been tossed around quite a bit. Someone else said your horns are very impressive." He snorted a laugh. "Oh my god you are *preening* right now."

"You don't think my horns are impressive?" I bit my lip as he rolled his eyes.

"No comment." He tucked his phone away. "So, what's the next step?"

I clicked my tongue as I let my brain kick around some ideas. "My thought is that these bastards have probably hit other fossil sites. And I also assume they couldn't have travelled far considering that when we first wake up, it's hard to move between forms. That Albertosaurus might still be in his big form."

"Yikes." Blaise cringed. "You think they're hiding a dinosaur somewhere? Like...where?"

"No idea." I shrugged, feeling a little helpless. "Maybe I'm right about the other sites, and maybe someone who works it might know something. Worth a shot, right?"

"You want to travel to other fossil sites in Canada? Don't

threaten me with a good time." He turned towards me, walking sideways. "I am going with you, right?"

I lifted my eyebrows. "After you put us on blast like that?"

"And helped you find the first major clue so far!" He skipped a bit to keep up with my stride. "I think we make a good team, don't you think, Mr. Kingston? How did you get him to think you were from the Field Museum, by the way?"

"Fake profiles and some light hacking. Easy stuff. The rest is confidence and charm." I pretended to dust my shoulder off. "Donatello swagger, baby."

"Lord." He rolled his eyes so hard I thought they'd fall out of his head. "Okay, Donny. Let me be your April O'Neil so we can take down these fossil-stealing Foot Clan fucks."

Oh.

Okay.

That made my big manly heart pitter-patter a bit.

Blaise smirked. "That totally worked, didn't it?"

"No." I sniffed.

I might have been in trouble with this guy.

Once we got back into town, we stopped for lunch and by my hotel room for my stuff before heading back to Blaise's little Airbnb. I made sure to update Montana on our lack of anything extremely concrete and sent Dalton a picture of a raptor eating an ice cream cone outside of a little frozen treat stand. I told him he should consider a neon blue look, since the frozen dairy-a-saurus was rocking the look well.

He sent me back a bunch of middle fingers and a big pink heart.

I munched on some apple chips while diving into anything I could find about fossil poaching or vandalism in the area. Sneaking into museum email chains and staff emails dropped a couple clues, but I also dug around for them notifying park rangers for suspicious people. Blaise tapped out messages on his phone, reaching out to any local paleontologists, volunteers, or science communicators that may have heard anything similar. He did this while touching up his eyeliner, which I found strangely fascinating.

"Hey, someone who works out in Brooks said they had someone cut a slice from a theropod femur about two weeks ago," Blaise said as he dusted some green mascara over his lashes. "That's about an hour from here."

I scrolled back over a chain of emails from a park in Maple Creek. Then backtracked to a ping to a local law enforcement office in Grand Prairie.

"Son of a bitch. They're hitting the fossil trail."

"What?" Blaise sat up, only one eye fixed with sparkly green makeup. "Are you serious?"

"Seems like it. I can't tell which direction they're coming from yet."

"The tracks from last night showed them heading east," Blaise said as he came to peek over my shoulder at my computer screen. "Who's on your background?"

Just when I thought he was almost perfect. He had to say something so telling of his lack of refinement for fine art.

"That's my husband Victor from *Yuri on Ice*." I left out the word "obviously" because of his raised eyebrow.

"Your husband is an anime figure skater?"

"Yes, Blaise. My husband is an anime figure skater who is a history maker." I tapped on my screen. "Stop gazing into his eyes and focus on the matter at hand."

"So, you're a big, Black, dinosaur shifter anime nerd? Am I missing anything?"

"Besides sexy, masculine, and brilliant?" I scoffed. "Only a couple hundred other adjectives that describe me, yeah."

Blaise shook his head with his eyes shut, as if he was trying to shake himself out of a haze.

I had that effect on men.

"Kay. Anyway. I bet if we follow the trail going east, we'll find more fossils getting hacked up."

"Worth a shot." I pulled up the map of the Canadian fossil trail. "Looks like we're heading out to Saskatchewan."

"Tonight?"

I shrugged and looked up at him where he hovered. "Why not?"

"Good. Because I'm actually supposed to be out of here by like five tonight."

"Then let's grab some snacks and hit the road." I shut my laptop and packed it away. "You have a car we can use?"

Blaise made a face that was a mix of amusement and apprehension. "Yeah. I do." The way he scrunched his nose started to make me nervous. "Sorry in advance."

BLAISE

Dolores wasn't the newest model of car in existence. And yeah, *technically,* she was older than I was both in actual age and modern expectations, but she had gotten me across the country with only minor issues. She was a great car. Just...sort of boxy and well...beige. But she had tons of space and the back seats were so comfortable.

So the fact that Royal, the *oh-so handsome, masculine* and *brilliant* man, erupted into laughter upon seeing my Dolores ruffled my feathers.

"Excuse you," I snapped. "You can walk if you have an issue with my car."

"You have a Chrysler Heritage? Jesus, this minivan is as old as I am, and I mean the fucking Cretaceous."

"Ha-ha." I unlocked the side door and slid it sideways so I could rearrange my life. Everything I owned was stuffed into Dolores, carefully arranged in small boxes and a handful of duffels. Most of it was clothes that I didn't care about, but I did have some treasures I didn't want squished. My wig case and costume chest being the things I didn't want touched by anyone else but myself.

After shoving some things aside and moving my backpack to the furthest backseat, I glared at Royal to see if he was done being a dick.

"Are you all giggled out now? Can we go?"

"Does this thing run on gas, or do you push it with your feet like the Flintstones?" He cracked a grin as he slipped into the passenger seat. He made a happy little gasp and touched the radio. "Oh my God. You have a cassette player in this. That's so advanced!"

"You're such an asshole," I said around an exhale, cranking my baby to life. Royal fiddled with my dial, and I slapped his hand. "Stop it."

"Do you have a tape in there? What do you jam to?"

"What do I jam to?" I sliced him with my side eye. "You and Dolores *are* the same age." He pretended to be mortally wounded as I plugged in my Bluetooth speaker into my cigarette lighter. "There's an old Garth Brooks tape that's wedged in there that came with the car. So, if you want to *jam*, play it through this."

"DJ Royal at your service." I heard his phone unlock and the telling rhythmic tapping of someone pecking out an app on their phone. "You didn't answer my question, though. What do you like to listen to?"

"I'm up for anything as long as it's not old country or screaming death metal." After a couple more clicks, some relaxed, lo-fi beats came through the small speaker, filling

Dolores with some decent ambient music. "So," I said after getting on the highway. "Would it be weird of me to ask you dinosaur questions? Like, is that rude or anything?"

Royal shook his head, leaning back in his seat. "Nah. Ask away."

"Okay." I drummed on the wheel with my fingers. "Did ceratopsians travel in herds?"

"Mm-hm. Big ones. Anywhere from twenty to forty strong. Bulls lead the herd, keeping them safe. Mommas and babies in the middle to keep them from getting picked off."

"Did you have a herd?" I glanced over to see him nod.

"I did. Since we could move between forms back then, I changed herds a lot. I bounced between a couple different ceratopsians and hadrosaurs and was an ankylosaur for a little bit. The Regaliceratops was the one that fit the best. I had my longest run as one of them. I think that's why it stuck after the asteroid impact."

I hummed, thinking about my next line of interrogation. "What about—uh." I hesitated and felt heat flood my cheeks. "Is there anything I *can't* ask?"

Royal sighed and rolled his head over to look at me, his expression unamused. "You're going to ask about the cloaca, aren't you?"

"For science!" I tried to relax my shoulders down, but they were stuck up around my ears.

"Uh-huh."

"It's a valid question about anatomy! Don't make it weird!"

"That fucking article, man. What did she say? Swiss army knife of buttholes?"

I couldn't stop the machine-gun laughter that popped out of me. I knew the article he was talking about, referencing the fossilized Psittacosaurus cloaca that was recently released to the press. My search history now included "Psittacosaurus Swiss

Army Butthole," and I was fairly sure I was on an FBI watch list.

"Well?" I managed around my laughter, which was stealing all of my breath. "Is it?"

"My butthole is none of your business."

"Oh, you cannot be a prude with me." I wiped a tear from my cheek. "I've seen your dick."

"But my butthole will remain a mystery." He flourished it with jazz hands, which nearly made me crash Dolores. "Next question."

"Ugh, you're no fun."

Royal smirked, just so proud of himself. The sun was starting to hang low in the sky; the late afternoon light painted his chestnut skin with a golden hue. His brown eyes almost looked deep red when the sunlight hit them, glowing like topaz in amber light.

It kinda hurt to look at him too long. Knowing that for a brief moment only a couple of nights ago, he was mine for a heartbeat. How epic would it be to have a hunky dinosaur boyfriend?

Oh, your boyfriend is a doctor. That's neat. Can he stab theropods with his nose?

But having a dinosaur friend was close. Right?

Were we friends? We had to have at least been that. You didn't go through a near miss with a Giganotosaurus without coming out as friends on the other side.

"Let's flip the script," he said after a couple beats. "Anything I can't ask *you*?"

"I'm not telling you about my butthole either," I snapped immediately.

"Not what I was going to lead with, but noted." He tilted his head towards my life, shoved into the backseats. "You moving?"

"Yes and no?" I winced. "I'm between places at the moment."

"So this is your ride and your pad, then?"

"Yep." I gave her a pat on the dashboard. "Living in style, exploring Canada and its endless fossil sites."

"That sounds like a good story." Royal watched the passing highway sign as he spoke, his body relaxed into the faded gray car seat. "You're bouncing between provinces and territories tracking down fossil sites for a job or just for the hell of it?"

"Both and neither." I laughed as he gave me a perplexed look. "I'm not being cagey. It's just complicated."

"Try me." He cocked a brow. "I dare you to be more complicated than my backstory."

"Different ballparks, Royal. I'm not a dinosaur—I'm a messy genderqueer darling who's in the middle of a life crisis. I'm interesting in the way a flaming dump truck of sparkles is entertaining."

Royal's smile could cause bones to melt, but his laugh was like a cannonball of delight. It was the sort of gut-deep, boisterous sound that ricocheted off everything in an explosion of happiness. It was impossible not to crack a grin when you were in the middle of the storm.

"I'm all about flaming disasters with sparkles. My brother Dalton and I once set up a glitter bomb to go off when someone sat on the toilet. There's still glitter on the ceiling in that bathroom."

"You two sound like a nightmare." I shook my head as he cackled.

"Yeah, we are. So tell me about your sparkly dumpster fire life. Warm me with your glittery fire. Oh." He sat up and looked over at me. "Shit, you said genderqueer. Do you have pronouns you prefer?"

Even though he was being nice, it still made my chest

tighten a bit to explain myself. I had gotten so used to puffing out my chest when people got combative about my *confusing* identity that hearing something kind felt foreign. It was like an atrophied muscle jerking back to life.

"Right now, I'm okay with he/him. I was they/them for a while, but...I'm leaning a little more femme male than nonbinary these days. Sorry, that's...probably weird."

"Nah. It's not. I'm old, but I'm not stuck in the past. I can adjust pronouns. Just let me know. Anyway, sparkle fire. Lay it on me."

I rubbed at the loosening knot in my chest with my palm as I spoke. "Jesus, where to begin with that. Well, I was working in a very dead-end job as a barista. I know, a twinky gay guy slinging coffee at a major chain coffee place known for friendly staff? Well, B, you are a *trendsetter*. But surprise, surprise, I got very sick of it. You ever have that moment when you're trying to make a quad-latte with soy, and you realize you fucking hate your life?"

"Hasn't everyone?" Royal supplied, his sarcasm the chef kiss of dry delivery.

"I realized," I continued, very aware of how much I was moving my hands around as I spoke, driving safety be damned. "While standing in a cramped little drive-through space, smelling like milk and depression, that the last time I was really, truly happy was in community college. I didn't have enough money to do more than two classes, so I picked something I would enjoy: cooking and geology."

"Nice combo," Royal agreed.

"Yeah, turns out I hate cooking, but geology was amazing. I had this awesome teacher who loved paleontology, and I connected with him immediately. He did consultation for oil companies to make sure they weren't digging into fossil beds and let me go out to a site he was working on. He was *so* cool.

Over the summer, he offered me an internship working with his company so I could get hands-on training doing actual paleontology. I was so happy."

"You couldn't get hired on?" he asked, turning his attention to me after looking out over the horizon.

My sigh deflated my whole body. "I couldn't give up my time at work. The internship was unpaid. I had to turn it down so I could eat."

"Damn." Royal winced. "I'm sorry. You don't have family that could've helped you out?"

"It's always been just my mom and me, and last I heard I think she's out in Nevada?" I tried to recall the last time we'd spoken, about three months back. "Vegas is in Nevada, right? She was heading to Vegas."

"Ah." Royal clicked his tongue. "So that's a no."

"That's a big no. Mom is a nomad." I waved my hand at my surroundings. "Pot meet kettle, I guess. But unlike her, I actually do want to settle down one day. I just haven't found my spot."

Royal thumbed through his playlist and selected some older hip-hop, bringing the beat up a bit as he spoke. "Dreams of being a paleontologist dashed, you had an existential crisis at work and decided to up and bail?"

I tilted my head back and laughed like a ThunderCat. "Oh, no, no. Dumpster fire, remember?"

"It gets *better*?" His grin was sharp across his face. "Do tell."

"In a flourish of drama, I quit. Well, I tried to quit, but the manager was outside smoking, and we were in the middle of a rush. So I finished my shift but left a *powerful* sticky note on her desk." I sucked in air between my teeth and added, "She actually didn't find it until after I picked up another shift when Taylor was sick. But after that, I for-real quit. *Then*," I paused to take a sip of my watered-down iced coffee, "I found out I was homeless."

"You found out you were homeless? How does one find out they're homeless? Powerful sticky note on your door and locks were changed?" Royal leaned his elbow out of the window and turned his face towards the breeze.

"Much more traumatizing," I admitted. "My 'roommate' had been pocketing my half of the rent and didn't actually pay for the apartment for two months. So I came home to all my shit outside, and Garret was long gone."

"I felt the air quotes around 'roommate.'" He side-eyed me. "Gar-bear wasn't just honest about the rent?"

"Oh, *Gar-bear* was plenty honest about how we were just friends. We were cohabitating fuck buddies for four months, and the last month before he fucked me over—not in the fun way—I found out about his baby momma. So." I hummed a little tone of still-brewing anger. "Not a big fan of Gar-bear."

"You were right about the fire. This is roaring, B."

"I never lie about drama, sweetheart. When I say it was a fire, it was a *fire*." With my story finally done, I leaned back into my seat and let my body relax. The hum of the road helped ease my excitement of recounting my miserable little life with flair. "So leaving wasn't so hard. It was either stay where I was and be miserable, or go for broke and ride this until the wheels fall off. I figured, why not go out and see the world a little? Check out those fossil sites I always wanted to see? Hell, maybe I can try my hand at doing science communication and see what happens?" I shrugged. "Better than what I was doing."

"That takes some guts, B. What do you do about money?"

"Sleep in my car and eat light." I looked at him and stage-whispered, "I know this is shocking, but I don't actually have a plan."

"Leaning into that sparkly dumpster fire hard, huh?"

"I'll go out with a bang, baby. And I guess it's going well. I mean, I met a dinosaur shifter and am embarking on a crazy, possibly suicidal mission to find another one." I tossed him a smirk. "It could be worse."

He mirrored my grin. "I thought you said this was the type of stuff you listed as 'don'ts.' You having a change of heart?"

"Road-tripping across the country to fossil sites and hunting down dinosaurs is fun. Fighting them is not fun. That's all you." I wagged my finger at him.

"Here we go," he said with a laugh.

"Not 'here we go.' You're the big beefy one who can turn into a dinosaur. I'm fun-sized compared to you."

"Well, agreed." He tipped his head in acknowledgement, which absolutely didn't make my stomach flip a little. The devilish grin that spread over his face made me do a double take.

"What?" I squeaked, not understanding why he was smiling like that until I heard the music. "Oh. Royal. No."

Not karaoke. Not karaoke in my van with an almost blown Bluetooth speaker.

And please. No Salt 'n' Pepa karaoke.

"Here I go, here I go, here I go again. Girls, what's my weakness?" He put his fingers to his ears and leaned my way.

I sighed. "Men."

Maybe this was a terrible idea.

CHAPTER SEVEN

ROYAL

I didn't know what Blaise was talking about. I sang beautifully.

After serenading him with some of my favorite classics, including "Bohemian Rhapsody" by our lords and saviors, I had to update Montana on what the plan was. His last email let me know a storm had delayed flights, so he was stuck in France for a while longer with no real timeframe on when he could leave.

Yu had touched base that he was in Japan tracking down some amber fossil leads and asked me to hunt down some files on a couple Yakuza bosses. He also asked me to research the name of an old poet who had a town named after him. Apparently, it was vital information, which meant he was bored and didn't want to google it himself.

That dude was really badass and had great stories, but he was also strange as hell.

Baha was still resting, and Dalton had sent pictures from one of their dinosaur tourist trap visits while they were on the road.

Did you know there's a dinosaur theme park in the United States that has dinosaurs reenacting scenes from the Civil War?

Well, it exists. And Dalton almost got thrown out for trying to climb the Pteranodon that Abe Lincoln was riding on.

When he asked how my trip was going, my long text chain was filled with gifs of kittens biting people and explosions.

Dalton: Sounds like my Friday night.

Royal: Yeah? You let theropods chew on your back these days?

Dalton: His name is Simon, and he's family now, Royal. OHANA MEANS FAMILY.

Royal: You nasty.

My phone lit up as he called me, and I answered it with, "You got mad because you couldn't find the gif you wanted, didn't you?"

"No, I just couldn't text and pee."

"I told you not to call me when you're peeing."

"No," he said sharply. "You said not to call you when I'm pooping. Pick one."

"You're all class, my man." I rubbed my eyes as I laughed. "How's the trip going?"

"Great! We're having a lot of fun. Simon got to talk to someone about shark teeth while we were waiting in line, so he's all cute and excited. How's your kinky theropod sex trip?"

"Not as advertised. Montana said it was in and out, super easy. Now I got bite-mark scars in my back that I will never be able to explain and a missing theropod lost in Canada. So, you know. Living the dream." I climbed out of the van as Blaise pulled into a gas station. My legs were stiff from sitting for an hour, and my stomach rumbled for a snack. I pulled the phone away from my mouth and leaned over to look at Blaise pumping gas. "Want something from inside?"

"Water and Twizzlers?" he asked hopefully. I gave him a salute and headed for the store.

Dalton gave a little gasp. "Who was *that*?"

"A friend." I strolled to the drink aisle in the little closet of a gas station and scanned the shelves for something crisp and carbonated.

"A *secret friend*?"

"Maybe." I plucked my choice and grabbed Blaise a bottle of water. "Go look up the handle Fossil Fiter, with no 'gh.'" My ear was filled with the dull thud of fingers across the surface of a phone.

"You're really into the pretty ones, aren't you?" Dalton sounded far from the phone, like he was still looking at the screen instead of holding it up to his head. "Wow. Simon! Look."

"Who's that?" Simon's voice was just as far away.

"Royal's boyfriend."

"Not boyfriend, just a friend," I corrected. "Hi, Simon."

"He's getting him candy at a gas station," Dalton said with a tone that suggested I was being ridiculous. "So, obviously they're a thing."

"What?" Poor Simon always sounded so confused.

"Oh, shit, Royal! Did this guy video you fighting the—oh. Ouch. *Ouch!*" Dalton hissed through his teeth, and I heard Simon gasp.

"Is that a Giganotosaurus?" Simon asked with pure delight. "Look at the skin coloring. How interesting."

"No, really. I'm fine. Your concern is embarrassing," I deadpanned, placing my items on the counter.

"Sorry, Royal," Simon said after a beat. "Are you okay?"

"He's fiiine," Dalton added like me being an appetizer wasn't a big deal. "Takes more than a big sharp tooth to hurt my Daddy Tops."

"Damn straight." I pushed through the door after paying and strolled back to Dolores. "Listen, man, keep this a secret from Montana for a while?"

"The video exposing not only that dinosaur shifters are real and the fact that one got the upper hand on you or the secret boyfriend?"

"Yes." I paused outside of Dolores, not getting inside with Blaise just yet. "And not a boyfriend."

"But y'all fucked, right?"

"Dalton," Simon scolded. "That's really none of our business."

"I don't kiss and tell," I said.

Dalton cackled. "Totally did. Ow, don't pinch my arm, Simon. Go *lower*."

"Bye, you two," I said around a laugh, ending the call before climbing into the van.

Blaise glanced my way as I got inside, lazily checking his phone. "I think your brother just followed me on social media. Icon is a raptor with a pink mohawk? Handle SexasaurusD?"

"That's the one." I passed him his requested snacks. "What did he say that gave him away?"

"He commented on my video that the triceratops was hot."

I laughed and took a swig of my drink. "Asshole." My phone buzzed, and I fished it out to check the message. "Someone out at the T.rex Center in Eastend said they'd chat with us."

"That's still like two hours out, and the sun is going down." Blaise crossed his arms over the wheel. "You wanna crash at a hotel? Go out there in the morning? Oh!" He sat up with a grin. "Will they let us check out the local fossil sites?"

"Slow your roll. Let me work my magic." I started typing away. "And yeah, let's find a place to crash."

While Dolores revved to life and Blaise pulled her onto the road, I shot our contact an email about timing tomorrow and requested a peek at the site. Even though I had been out to Canada many times, I'd never visited the center before. It was rare I got to experience new things these days, so visiting a new center was actually pretty exciting.

The hotel Blaise found was a decent chain with all the modern benefits. The beds were promised to be clean, free cable, an indoor pool that was probably closed, and a mediocre breakfast that would taste decent first thing in the morning. Since Blaise had made it very clear we were not going to be "complicating" things, I made sure to ask for two beds in the room.

I should have asked for two bathrooms because Jesus Christ did that man pamper himself before bed. He spent two hours in the bathroom showering and doing this skin care regimen he insisted was *critical* for his existence. I was not proud to say I went out into the parking lot to piss because that small, delicate Venus flytrap nearly clawed my face off when I tried to go in there to use the facilities.

He looked so unassuming in his lounge pants that sat low on his hips, a towel wrapped around his head, and a lime-green mask of slime on his face. The most impressive part of it all was how he could still eat over half of a large pizza while being so small and not smudge his mask.

"How's your back?" he asked from his bed around a bite of pizza. I was in the middle of changing into something to sleep in, so I went to the mirror and tried to look at my bare back in it.

"Sore. But it doesn't look angry anymore."

Blaise stuffed the last bit of crust into his mouth and walked over, eying my chew marks. I let the smaller man turn me around and apply some cold antiseptic to the wounds, the cold bite stinging before it soothed over the ache.

"There." He wiped off his hands. "They're looking better. Do you heal faster than humans?"

"I don't think so." I shrugged, turning back around to face him. "But maybe a little faster."

He hummed, then cleared his throat. "Well, you're not infected, so you're fine."

He disappeared into the bathroom again, so I finally crawled into bed. After a moment, I heard the door open, and he spoke. "Hey, Royal?"

I bit back a yawn and looked his way. "Yeah?"

Blaise's towel around his hair was gone, his hair wild and tousled. The face mask had been wiped away, and the light behind him made the dark strands of his hair almost red. His mouth twisted as he nibbled on his lip, his arms crossing over his chest as he leaned against the doorframe.

"Um." He shook his head, a strand of hair flopping down on his cheek. He swept it back quickly. "I have a friend out at the Regina branch of the Royal Saskatchewan Museum who could probably get us in to see the fossils there."

"That's great."

"Yeah." He tapped his finger on his arm, then turned and moved back into the bathroom. "Goodnight."

"Night," I called back after him.

I guess the poor guy had too much pizza or something.

CHAPTER EIGHT

BLAISE

"How do you do that?"

"Do what?" I blinked a couple times to make sure the false eyelashes stayed in place before taking my last bite of waffle.

"Glue shit to your eyelids and eat at the same time."

"Practice. And working retail for my entire adult life means I'm hardwired to eat while multitasking." I scanned over my eyeliner choices before landing on teal since it went better with my scarf. The exceptionally crappy night of sleep I had meant I had to up my makeup game for the day. I couldn't quite decide if I was anxious about chasing down living dinosaurs or how I was a chickenshit about Royal.

I had almost worked up the courage to try and flirt with him last night. After being in the car all day with him, laughing and chatting, I felt like we had at least a small connection. But I couldn't help but question every bit of it.

My track record for projecting my feelings on other people was astronomically bad. Each time I had been so confident that someone was into me, it was because I was lonely or smitten. Or both, if we're being honest. Being jobless, basically friendless, and shacking up with a really, *really* attractive guy with a great personality and large portions all around was definitely making me pathetically smitten.

Could I probably get another round out of him or at least a rerun of the night at the club with him?

Yeah, probably. There's no guy who would turn down a blowjob.

But I was fairly sure the aftermath of his apathy would crush my soul.

I shoved all that away in my mental chest of sad Blaise emotions. "Did your contact get back with you?"

"Yep. We're good to tour the place and see the site. I'm hoping we get a chance to see the carved-out fossil to see if it matches what we've seen. Maybe we'll get lucky, and they saw someone suspicious." He scrolled through his laptop as he ate. We had both been a little too excited about the waffle press in the lobby, and Royal had burned his first two attempts. His next five did okay, though.

"It's a museum. They would have security cameras, wouldn't they?"

Royal nodded, finishing his last bite. "That's my hope." He stood and shut his laptop, stuffing the thing into his bag. The shirt he was wearing was strained across his torso, and I became mildly obsessed with watching his forearms flex as he tucked the small computer away.

The drive out to the discovery center was a long stretch of open country with wide, open sky. Royal played music on low, thankfully sparing me from random karaoke for the time being. The low rhythm of the music and hum of the engine was soothing, and it was surprisingly cozy to drive in comfortable silence as the sun warmed the crisp spring air.

The area around the T.rex center might have looked barren and boring to most, but to me, it was surrounded by opportunities. The center was a small smile of shining windows across the base of large earthy hills, no doubt teeming with more fossils yet to be discovered. In the front garden, a disjointed cast of a T.rex skeleton lay on its ribs, the head floating a couple feet from the torso. It almost looked like the dinosaur was doggy-paddling towards the entrance to snap its jaws at guests.

I parked Dolores in visitor parking and basically cart-wheeled out of the van. I couldn't wait to get inside and see the place, since it was a new museum I hadn't visited yet. Royal chuckled as I started snagging pictures of the building and weird T.rex out front.

"Are you laughing at my excitement?" I zoomed in on the teeth of the skeletal animal greeting us.

"I'm chuckling in amusement at your enthusiasm. Want me to take a picture of you by the T.rex?"

"Nah, I got it." I grinned at my camera as I flipped it around, making sure to get the goofy rex in the picture. To Royal's credit, he didn't give me any hell for retaking it four times before I was satisfied.

Across the doors, a sign announcing that the museum was closed for some light renovations nearly sank my heart, but a smiling face opened the door just as we got close enough to see the sign.

"You must be Blaise and Royal," the man said, holding the door open for us. He wore a museum polo and jeans, thinning hair slicked back and laugh lines bursting from his grin. "I'm Tom. C'mon in."

"I appreciate you letting us check this place out while it's closed, Tom." Royal shook his hand, and I did the same before stepping inside. It almost felt like I was a kid getting away with skipping school or sneaking into a place I wasn't supposed to be in. Normally, this place would have been alive with light and activity, no doubt brimming with children's voices and excitement. Our footsteps echoed, Tom's voice carrying further than it normally would with no other noises to dampen it.

"So you're doing a story on the fossils getting vandalized across Canada?" Tom didn't even bother locking the door behind us, but instead led us in to look around.

"Yeah." Royal stuffed his hands in his hoodie pockets as he scanned the place. "Apparently there's an issue with people cutting slices from them lately?"

"Slices, huh?" Tom furrowed his brows. "You know, we had a gash taken out of one of our T.rex femurs a couple weeks back."

"A long rectangle?" I prompted, and he nodded. "Something out in the field? Or from the prep lab?"

"It must have happened in the field because I can't imagine it happening in-house. None of our volunteers would have done that." Tom shook his head. "Strangest thing, really. Why would they cut rectangles?"

"Any new volunteers to the team?" Royal tried, but Tom shook his head. "Strange people around?"

"It's a museum," Tom laughed. "We get all kinds here. But the fossil lab is monitored, and we have cameras. I think we would have seen someone come in and out. Oh." He pulled his phone from his pocket and excused himself, stepping away to answer it.

Royal stepped in closer to me, speaking in a low tone. "I need to get to that security tape."

"I don't think he's going to let you see that."

"I know. I need to go sneak off to find it. Probably get to their computer system." Royal's brown eyes swept the cameras posted up in the corners before landing back on me. "Think you can distract him for a bit?"

"You're going to break into this sweet little museum's

computer system? Are you insane?" I snapped. "I like this place, and Tom is actually nice!"

"I'm not going to mess anything up. If whoever was at the site the other day made a move here, we might be able to find something useful."

I tried to expel the anxiety from my soul with the deepest sigh I could muster. "If you get us thrown out of here before I get to see Scotty, I will end you."

"Scotty?" Royal gave me a confused look that morphed into surprise as I glared at him.

"The complete T.rex skeleton this museum is known for. How are you the dinosaur in this situation?" I didn't mean for it to come out as a hiss, but I may as well have arched my back like a cat as I spoke to him.

Royal made a little X over his heart. "I won't keep you from your darling T.rex."

"Better not." I beamed a smile at Tom as he walked back over to us. "Tom, I would love to do an interview with you while we tour the place if that's alright. I brought my hand mic and selfie stick, so we can do this in style."

"Yeah, I'd love to!" Tom smiled.

"I'm going to excuse myself to the restroom, guys. I'll catch up with you." Royal gave his stomach a rub, his face wincing just slightly. "Don't wait up."

"Down the hall there to your right." Tom pointed, and Royal nodded, making his escape. I kept my smile in place as I dug out my equipment from my backpack, but my heart was pounding.

Keep cool, Blaise. Royal knows what he's doing.

ROYAL

I HAD NO IDEA WHAT I WAS DOING, BUT IT WAS WORTH A shot.

Breaking into places was more of a Dalton or Yu thing. I was usually the guy waiting outside helping them navigate the security system and killing the silent alarm. Stealth wasn't my specialty, but I didn't have a lot of options. I was way too brawny to be a ninja. Beggars couldn't be choosers, I guess.

The museum wasn't a massive place, so finding the main office wasn't hard to do. The only issue was that getting to said goal required me to pass through a couple showrooms being prepped for new exhibits. Making a fast exit wasn't going to be an option, so I had to make sure to keep the noise down.

Tom seemed to be the only staff on site, which helped tip the odds of me being discovered in my favor. It also helped that the staff didn't deem it necessary to lock doors since the place wasn't currently open to the public. I had a lockpick set, but I really sucked at it.

The office that held all the goodies was a simple room with a modest desk, shelves stacked with books, and various frames on the walls. Some held degrees, others were dated photos of people kneeling around fossils, and a smattering were crayon-drawn thank you letters from kids. Old book smell made the place calm and comforting, and I wanted nothing more than to start going through the shelves of paleontology books instead of breaking into their security system.

But work was work. And I had a theropod to find.

The old desktop whirred to life as I powered it on, the screen lighting up with the museum's logo and a lock screen. Now, in the movies, this was when I would do some fancy finger work and somehow figure out the password. Maybe there would be a handy sticky note or a picture with a date that would be the perfect Rosetta stone for this mystery.

I prefer to go in the backdoor.

In all the ways that implies.

I pulled a cable from my pocket, plugged in my phone to the computer's tower, and did what I like to call the old Royal Razzle Dazzle.

That's what I call the program I use to break PC security systems and get access to hard drives. And wouldn't you know it, it worked like a charm. The computer not only unlocked but gladly poured all of its information out for me to find.

The security cameras around the museum had a digital feed that was recorded on a cloud server. Getting access to that was a cakewalk, and I was able to start browsing immediately. Most of the videos were mundane, the same set of bodies coming and going during off hours. I skimmed through days with visitors, poked around through the feed with volunteers picking away at fossils or setting up new exhibits. Nothing stood out for days, and I was beginning to think that Tom was right about the fossil being desecrated before it made its way to the museum.

Until I spotted him.

The fucker thought he was being slick wearing the museum polo, but he wasn't anyone I was used to seeing in the group. He slipped in just after hours, using the front door with what looked like a key. Onyx curls swept back, tanned skin. He was a good-looking thief, I'd give him that. Obviously, he was someone who was used to being in control because he moved with the confidence of an apex predator as he made his way through the small museum.

"Son of a bitch." I rubbed at my mouth to keep from yelling as I watched this asshole stroll into the prep lab, pull some of the T.rex bones from the fossil cabinet, and take out his tools. It was over in a flash, his movements practiced and comfortable.

A perfect rectangle carved right out of the bones.

I took my time snagging some freeze-frame shots of his face, but the distance the cameras were from him made the picture muddy and a little pixelated. But it was better than nothing. The fact that an alarm never went off after this asshole walked in meant they had someone manipulating the security system from behind the scenes. Maybe someone at the museum, but likely they had their own Guy In The Chair doing their own razzle dazzle.

They were organized. And good at what they did.

But so was I.

After I got what I needed, I closed out of everything and put it back the way I found it. The computer was locked back up, my phone disconnected, and the computer powered down. I even made sure to put the chair I was sitting in back the way it was before I sat down and slipped out of the office like a handsome ghost.

Just as I was making my way down the hall to meander back out to find Tom and Blaise, the sound of footsteps ahead of me made me freeze. Two people were chatting about the delivery time for a new model being brought in, walking my direction towards the office. I spun around quickly, darting into one of the showrooms to hide. The idea was to duck behind one of the life-sized reconstructions of my ancestors so they could pass, but I don't have that sort of luck.

The way the showroom was laid out, there were two entryways to allow for staff and visitors to come and go as they please. Staff doors were painted like the backdrop of a Cretaceous forest with a sign warding off curious guests from peeking, blending in to not shatter the illusion. The visitor doors were propped open, ready to allow awestruck guests to gaze on the majesty of the ancient world.

Behind me, the two staff members' voices were just on the other side of the painted doors. Down the hallway leading to the guest doors, Blaise's chipper voice was echoing across the walls, heading my direction.

There was no damn good reason for me to be in that room. I was supposed to be indisposed in the bathroom, not hiding in the dark behind a pudgy hadrosaur.

If they found me here, it would definitely not be good.

Shit, shit, shit.

Why did I have to be such a big dude? If I was smaller, I would have just tried to duck down and hide in the fake ferns or post up behind one of the big fake dinosaurs. Hell, I would even try and crawl under a sauropod belly if I thought that would do anything.

Blaise and Tom were getting closer, their shadows playing across the walls as they turned down the hallway. The voices behind me almost sounded like they stopped just outside of the door I came from, laughing away at their delightful fucking day while I had a panic attack. All these big, fake dinosaurs and nowhere to hide.

I was screwed. This was it.

This was why you didn't send your IT guy into stealth missions! I was just too thick and pretty to hide! Montana was going to kill me. Getting caught on a viral video was one thing, but this? Hell, I may as well have just stayed in my dinosaur form. It was better than having to deal with the police.

Then it hit me.

The most stupid, dumbass, brilliant idea came into my head. It was such a bad idea that I almost laughed out loud at it.

Because you can either be terrified of bad ideas or be a boss and nail them.

Tom's voice was so close I could recognize that he was talking about plans for the new layout as I began to strip. My boots were shoved behind some fake plants, my jeans, sweater, and boxers shoved behind a fat baby ankylosaur crawling out of an egg. My shift was as quiet as it could be. The crack of my bones echoed so loudly in the small space I was convinced someone had heard it. But there was no pause in the conversation, and I didn't hear any of the staff members gasp in horror.

This was so stupid.

Gazing at the big, open mouth of a fake tyrannosaur through my shifted eyes was quite the experience, like a strange Twilight Zone episode. The dagger-lined maw was so familiar but not quite right. It didn't stink of death at all. More like old paint and dust.

I did my best to play the role I was destined to play: the formidable foe to the mighty King of the Dinosaurs as the showroom light clicked on.

I held my breath and froze.

"In this room we're going to be showing off more of the fleshed-out reconstructions along with the skeletons. These are going to be specifically Canadian-found dinosaurs. Oh, look at that." Tom's voice lifted in surprise as he spoke. "I didn't know we were getting in a Regaliceratops. This guy is new."

My eyes were gazing up at the fake T.rex, but I could hear them walking around me before sliding into my peripheral vision. Tom looked fascinated, his brows pressed down as he studied me like, well, a museum exhibit.

Blaise was staring at me like I just insulted his mother and choice of fashion in one breath.

"It looks really good, doesn't it?" Tom cooed. "Interesting coloring choices. The rust-colored bands on the legs are a nice touch. And of course, the red frill looks great."

Tom's face got uncomfortably close to my left eye. I could practically see the man's nose hairs as he scanned over my face, his fingers touching my cheek.

It was already hard not to blink, but his body wash was powerful this close to my face. The stinging, tickling sensation inside of my nose was growing stronger.

Another poke at my face. "Cheeks. Huh. I've never seen a reconstruction of ceratopsians with cheeks. That's amazing."

"Does it look amazing?" Blaise bit out. "Looks a little bloated and fake, don't you think? Like a fat, overly sure of himself bull that maybe didn't think through his choices before he landed in the situation he was in?"

That little shit.

Fuck I really needed to sneeze. My eyes started to water. My lungs burned from holding my breath. This may have been a mistake.

"Uh, sure." Tom hedged. "I guess. I think it looks nice." Tom's dry hand landed on my beak, trailing up to touch my nose horn. Why was this guy so handsy? And *why* did he slather himself in body wash? He smelled like an Old Spice truck crashed into his shower.

Oh God please go. I'm going to die.

As Tom moved around to inspect my other side, Blaise glared at me. I let my eye flick to him, and he mouthed, "OH MY GOD," his cheeks flushed and dark brows down in absolute horror. I tried to send vibes of "help" and "get fucking Tom out of here before I sneeze everywhere" with the look on my face, but it's hard to read emotion on a dinosaur's face unless you are one. We have chronic resting badass face. Blaise continued to look pissed.

I winked.

He flipped me off.

Tom was getting increasingly touchy as he walked the length of my body. I shot Blaise a look as I felt Tom kneel down to check my undercarriage, and Blaise snickered at my misfortune.

"Pretty realistic, huh?" Blaise called out, never taking his eyes off me. Smug little bastard. I wanted so badly to stick my tongue out at him in protest, but I didn't dare move. Especially when a strange paleontologist was so close to parts of my anatomy I wanted to remain a mystery.

Then it happened.

All at once.

Tom touched my belly. I inhaled sharply in surprise, which triggered the brewing storm in my nose, and I exploded phlegm all over the fake T.rex.

Blaise yelped and covered his mouth, Tom slammed his head against my gut as he scrambled up and away from me, and the room descended into a very awkward silence.

"W-was that—" Tom stammered, and Blaise snapped into action.

"Got you!" Blaise gave a strained, mildly insane witch laugh. He held up his phone, nearly dropping it as he waved it around. "I played the sound of a...hippo sneezing into a megaphone."

"That was *you*?" Tom sounded offended and afraid. "That scared the shit out of me!"

Blaise made a long, strangled laugh pour from his lips, and he gave Tom two finger guns. "The look on your face!"

Tom took a shaky breath and rubbed his chest. "Yeah, that was, um...great. Please don't do that again."

With the sneeze gone, I could smell the waves of anxiety mixed with fine drops of sweat from Blaise. The way his cheeks and neck flushed was a massive sign of how embarrassed he was.

"Sorry, Tom," he said around a fake laugh. "Just having some fun."

Tom nodded and exhaled. "Let me show you the rest of the showroom. Then we should probably find your friend."

"Yep. Totally." Blaise shot me a look from hell before trotting after Tom.

Whoops.

CHAPTER NINE

BLAISE

"Are you out of your fucking mind?"

For such an intimidating, large specimen of a man, Royal could look properly ashamed of himself. He had killer puppy dog eyes and knew how to use them, which made yelling at him very difficult.

After Tom's blood pressure went back down, he finished up the tour, a bit more rushed than before. Royal found us near the gift shop, and I was fully convinced that Tom now hated my guts. When I asked about seeing the fossil site, he said, "Maybe another time."

"I'm so pissed at you," I continued, cranking Dolores's engine. "Tom thinks I'm such an asshole now."

"I found the security footage," he mumbled like a scolded child trying to apologize.

"Great."

Big brown eyes aimed up at me from under his lashes.

"Stop it." I stabbed him with my best scowl. "The big doe eyes aren't going to work on me."

"I got pictures of the guy carving out chunks of fossils." His voice was low and somber. "I can run his face against some facial recognition software to get a match." He sighed. "If you're not too disappointed that I sneezed on Scotty."

"Oh my God," I rubbed at my forehead to fight back the headache.

"I know how much you like meat-eaters."

"Royal." I tried to sound sterner, but the fucker made me laugh.

A brilliant grin split his face. "You laughed, so I'm not in trouble anymore."

"That is not at all how this works."

"I don't make the rules." His big shoulders shrugged.

"I thought your dinosaur form was this sacred, super top-secret thing. So far, I've seen you whip it out twice now." I shot him a look. "You're a shifter hussy."

"I panicked!" he barked around a laugh. "It worked, didn't it?"

"Barely! And you got felt up by a middle-aged man, so. If that's a win to you, then God bless." I dismissed him with a wave of my hand. "Now I know your type."

"I'm pansexual, baby. I got lots of types."

I hated how easily he coaxed a laugh from me. Even with all of this stress, he was still having a good time. I envied the hell out of that. His deep chuckle and cheeky smirk cracked through the veneer I kept trying to paint over my platonic feelings for him. Royal was slowly killing me.

"We're heading to Regina next." I finally spoke. "My friend Laila works there as an exhibit assistant while she's getting her master's. This is actually the first time I'll get to meet her in person." I paused and gave him a long look. "No whipping forms out there or getting us thrown out, okay? I like her."

"Cross my heart."

I hummed, not convinced. Royal plugged in the Bluetooth

speaker and got some music going, and we relaxed into his mix of tunes for the drive.

"So." I bit into the some of the last bit of my candy reserve. "Speaking of types. You've been a human for a while now. Any epoch-long romances in your past?"

"Nah."

"Oh, please." I scoffed openly at his non-answer and offered him candy to help coax a better one from him. "There had to be someone along the way. Don't be coy."

"I didn't really have romances way back in the day. I had mates and my herd, lots of little calves to carry my bloodline. As a human..." He trailed off, his face scrunching. "Since we don't age, it makes it hard to really let yourself connect with anyone."

"You don't age?" I gave him a onceover. "Like, at all?"

"I don't think so. That or we're like elves and age really slowly."

"Nerd," I teased, and he flipped me off.

"Says the man who tripped over himself to get a selfie with a dead dinosaur."

"Scotty is an icon. Anyway." I waved my hand to dismiss the topic. "Your aging is nebulous. Are you worried it'll be like a vampire situation? Like you outlive the ones you love and grow distant and hardened over time?"

"Exactly." Royal nodded, the playfulness in his tone fading. "My brother Dalton is dating a human, and I asked him about that exact thing. I asked him what he would do when Simon grows old and dies, but he's still standing. He said that he just wants to love him as hard as he can until that time comes and not dwell on it. Until then, he wants to have Simon and his family and figure it out along the way."

The sticky candy in my mouth lost some of its flavoring. "That idea scares the shit out of me."

"How so?" Big brown eyes met mine for just a moment as I

pulled my gaze from the road. Curiosity was painted all over his face, like he was hopeful I had some secret insight.

"I just mean having someone love me until the end. It sounds defeatist, I guess, but I've never had anyone stick by me. My mom bailed years ago, my boyfriends have been jokes, and my friends are flighty at best. I don't know if I'd know how to handle someone who'd love me for decades. Especially a whole damn family."

Royal tilted his head in thought. "Fair. I think allowing yourself to be vulnerable enough to be loved is what's scary."

"After a certain amount of time getting your heart stepped on, you stop remembering how to be vulnerable," I mumbled. "You just expect the inevitable. They leave."

"Everything ends, B." Royal shrugged. "I've seen a couple mass extinctions now. The world has ended several times over. I've seen my calves grow up and die. Hell, we had a member of our team die. Reaper. I'd never felt grief like that before."

"I'm sorry." I offered him more candy, and we both munched on the sugary goodness for a while. "How did he die?"

"Shot. We trusted the wrong people, and he got killed during a fossil heist. He was Montana's...I dunno. Mate? Husband? Not sure what label they had. Reaper was like a big brother. It fucked us all up when he wasn't there anymore." Royal licked his lips, pulling the bottom one into his teeth for a moment. "But I don't regret having known him. Having loved him as much as I did. It hurt so bad when he died, but thinking about him makes me hopeful. Happy. Maybe that's what Dalton meant about loving Simon as much as he does."

"That's kinda beautiful." I picked at Dolores's steering wheel, trying to ignore the tightening in my chest. "Makes me hopeful."

"Me too."

I decided not to ask about his past flings after that conversation, mostly because my heart was floating in a vat of unnamed emotions. Each song that rolled over in Royal's playlist seemed to toss my head into different strings of thought, from mortality to heartbreak.

We stopped for snacks and a restroom break before we finally arrived in Regina, surprised to find the museum absolutely popping. The bright distraction helped me shake loose from my haze, and I latched onto it with both hands. A massive science-themed fair was in full swing, a bright mix of STEM games to teach people some basic science fundamentals set in a carnival atmosphere. The smell of popcorn and fried sugar mixed in the air with the joyful sounds of people playing and learning.

I loved it immediately.

"Did your friend mention this place was having a fair today?" Royal slipped from Dolores after I parked, following me as I walked around to the back of the van.

"She failed to." I pulled the trunk doors open and started going through my luggage. "But she's probably super busy and didn't think about it."

"Looks fun." Royal leaned on the door, watching the carnival before studying me. "What are you doing?"

"Looking for something to wear."

"You look fine." He gestured towards me. "What's wrong with that?"

"Ugh." I shoved a chest aside and pulled a duffle over. "I look like I've been driving all day. I want to change shirts and freshen up."

Royal lifted his brows and didn't comment, keeping his place near the door like he was guarding the van. As I tugged a new shirt on and reapplied some deodorant, he tilted his head towards the chaos of cases stockpiled in the back of Dolores.

"Are those wig cases?"

"Yup." I smoothed my shirt down and looked for my lip gloss. When he reached for one, I slapped his hand.

"There's like four wig boxes back here."

"I know," I sighed, the ache resurfacing. "I had to give four others away. And my costumes are drastically lacking now too. I don't even want to talk about my shoes."

I allowed Royal to peek into my costume chest. Then he swung his head towards me.

"You're a drag queen?"

"I *was*," I corrected, trying to not sound bitter. "Hard to construct an act when you're homeless and have mostly second-hand costumes that are a bit too big."

He snapped his hand back as I went to slap it away from another wig case. I finished freshening up and shut the doors. Laila responded to the text I sent her letting us know she'd be free closer to lunch, but to enjoy the fair until then.

I nodded towards the fair. "Do you want to check it out or grab lunch?"

"Both. I smell cotton candy, and that's all I want now."

"Surprise, surprise." I fell in step with him. "You want a mountain of sugar? I'm so shocked."

He stacked his hands under his chin in a fake pose of mock cuteness. "It's because I'm so sweet."

I rolled my eyes so hard I saw my own ass, and Royal rewarded me with one of his chuckles. It was hard to pretend it didn't give me butterflies.

The fair was even better up close. The games were run by museum staff, challenging kids and adults alike to race with magnets, build circuit boards, make slime, or play dinosaur guessing games. There were more classic carnival games sprinkled in, along with overly cheesy signs, and of course tons of fried food.

While most of the games were geared for younger people, I

did learn a couple things at that carnival. For example, Royal could eat three bags of cotton candy by himself, and the man has a vicious competitive streak. I learned this when I beat him at ring toss, and he demanded two rematches.

Demanded. Man was sixty-five million years old, and he demanded a ring toss rematch.

"You are *pouting*," I pointed out as we moved to the next game.

"You cheated."

"Can't cheat at ring toss, Royal."

"Apparently you can, and you did." He narrowed his brown eyes at me. "I'm onto you, Blaise Fite. If I knew your middle name, I'd have done the whole thing."

"Blaise is my middle name. My first name is awful, and you aren't even close to learning my ways, Royal...do you have a last name?" I stole a piece of his cotton candy he was still working on.

"No. We were named after our species or the formation our holotypes were found in. I usually go by Kingston when I have to make something up." He tore into the pink cloud he was holding with his teeth. "What's wrong with your first name?"

"This conversation has officially segued." I passed him a mallet and pointed to the massive stuffed, green T.rex lounging beside the game. "Hit the pad at the base of the tower and make that little puck ring the bell at the very top. I want that T.rex."

Royal wrinkled his nose and lifted his chin towards the prizes. "But there's a much cuter triceratops right there."

"That's for people who can't hit hard enough. The T.rex is the grand prize, and that's what I want." I poked his arm, which was like nudging a boulder. "Put these to use."

Royal sighed, spinning the mallet in his hand as he walked up to the carnival game. The attendant looked a little nervous as Royal gave the rickety old game a onceover. He didn't even put down his cotton candy as he reared his tree-trunk arm back like he was going to clobber the damn thing through the earth. Just before he crashed the mallet down into the pad like the thing offended his mother, he eased up just enough to send the puck a little over halfway up.

Royal looked so proud of himself as he plucked the small little powder-blue triceratops from the prize wall and handed it to me.

I glared at him.

But I took it.

I also took a piece of his cotton candy when he offered me some. Cute bastard.

ROYAL

THIS WAS THE FIRST TIME I HAD EVER BEEN TO A CARNIVAL, and I had no idea that science-themed ones even existed.

Montana rarely unleashed us on a place that had the means for us (mainly Dalton) to get into trouble, so things like large public events were often avoided. But this was a blast. The games were fun, I actually learned some stuff, and the food was overly processed spools of heaven.

Above all, I was enjoying spending time with Blaise.

Yeah, he was a brat and gave me shit on a constant basis. He also was a cheat at ring toss and always looked a little annoyed. But he was fun. I liked his dagger side-eyes and little smirks he tried to hide. I liked that he was a fussy mess with a van filled with costumes and followed the beat of his own drum. The more I got to know him, the more I liked him.

It didn't help that I also knew how succulent his mouth was. And what he sounded like when he came. Those memories tangled with his bright personality was making me crush on the guy hard. Really hard. More than once, I had to walk myself back from wanting to take his hand or comment on how nice he looked. For a brief moment when he was cheating at ring toss, I almost kissed his cheek.

I couldn't, though. He had drawn the line in the sand earlier, and I had to respect that.

Don't complicate things. We're just friends.

I could be his friend. Hell, I really liked being his friend.

These thoughts were rattling around in my head as I followed him back to Dolores, and I realized that I was drooling over how nice his ass looked in his jeans. Not a friend thing to do. Stop looking at his ass.

Stop it.

For real, stop.

Damn, I bet I could bounce a quarter off those. Play them like little bongos.

Blaise turned and looked at me with a look of confused amusement, and for a hot second, I thought I said that out loud.

"What?" I said quickly and obviously guilty.

"I asked if you wanted to go get real food since all you had was pure sugar?" He eyed me as he opened the driver side door. "Are you slipping into a diabetic coma from all that candy?"

"Uh." I shook my head. "I thought you said your friend was free for lunch?"

He set his little triceratops on the driver's seat. "Yeah, that's true. Maybe she can eat with us." He shut the door and leaned on it, looking back towards the carnival. "I'm just getting hungry."

"I bet she won't be much longer." I watched him watching the carnival, admiring how a rogue curl always seemed to spiral right above his eyebrow. The fading green dye in his hair was lighter now, desperately needing a touchup that would likely never happen. A fleck of dirt from the wind had caught in the strand, and I reached out to pluck it before I could stop myself.

The moment I touched his hair, he blinked his eyes at me. The intent to remove the dirt evaporated, and instead, I brushed the strand back in a much more intimate gesture. My brain was trying to hit the brakes, sparks flying from the friction of logic crashing against emotion.

Hazel eyes danced over my face, the pupils expanding ever so slightly. I was back at the club again, watching those same eyes hooded, flashing lights around us, his tongue lapping over his bottom lip.

His fingers curled around my nape as I kissed him, pressing him back against the door. Lips caught mine, plucking and teasing as I smoothed my thumb over his jawline. Jesus, he was soft, his mouth tinted with sugar and hair smelling like citrus soap. Without the haze of alcohol, I could appreciate his flavor so much more. I could catch the small, subtle mannerisms of his kiss that were lost in the passion of the night at the club.

I had never had a kiss quite like this one. Blaise stole my breath with each touch of his lips, his fingers on the back of my neck like electric pulses against my skin. I was lost in it, happily drowning in it, and I refused to come up for air.

The drive to lift him up by his thighs so I could pin him to the van pulled me closer, but he broke the kiss with an exhale. Our noses brushed together, and I tilted my chin to dive in again, when his hand fell to my chest and lifted me out of the moment. Blaise swallowed, his other hand fishing out his phone.

"Laila texted." He cleared his throat, his voice sounding tight. "She said she's free now."

The small push of his palm against my chest was like a Mack truck slamming into me. Blaise didn't look up as he stepped around me and smoothed his hair back.

"We shouldn't keep her waiting."

"Yeah." I wiped off my lips.

What do I say now? Sorry? I fucked up? Can that be considered a friend kiss? Is that a thing?

Guilt stormed me as I followed him towards the museum. He told me we were friends, and I stomped over that because I couldn't keep myself reeled in. I was better than that. Frustration brewed in the pit of my stomach.

I used to be so good at this. In my other life, there wasn't a mate that wouldn't have me. I was powerful, a good protector, and kept my herd and mates safe. Now, as a human? I couldn't be trusted to handle the simplest request of keeping my sex drive in check.

I may have ruined a great friendship and the only other person here to help me with these damn fossil thieves.

I royally fucked up.

That's a painful but accurate phrase for this exact situation.

CHAPTER TEN

BLAISE

I felt like a ghost floating into the museum.

Numb. Transparent. Desperately hoping that the kiss I just had wasn't the cause of my death, but it felt like it was.

The moment Royal's lips touched mine, I knew in my now-dispelled soul that I could never have a casual fling with him. In novels they described kisses like electrical storms or feeling sparks flying. But that wasn't a storm. That was an earthquake. The ground shifted under me, and I felt the desperate sensation of knowing there was no control. At any moment, the shaking would tear down my life and leave it in shambles, and all I could go was hold on.

God, I wanted to hold on tight.

The only saving grace I had was the cellphone buzzing in my pocket, giving me a brief window of safety to escape from.

The problem, though, was that Royal's earthquake kiss already shook me down. A very real, very painful crack had raced right through me. Any fleeting thought of swiveling our platonic friendship to a sexy one was gone.

If he kissed me like that again, I was a goner.

Hell, I already might have been. When this was all over, and it would be in a matter of time, I didn't know if I'd ever be the same.

Ceratopsians would break your heart. Momma never warned me about that.

I was able to sift past my heartache to take in how beautiful the Royal Saskatchewan Museum was. The courtyard outside had already blown me away, with the gorgeous rainbow of flowers leading up to the doors. Inside, fairgoers were trickling in to see the exhibits after having fun playing games. The noise of voices hummed through the place, and the wide windows let the spring sunlight warm the tiles.

I spotted Laila immediately. She looked just like her profile picture she had of her grinning next to a Dunkleosteus. Not only had I made a fast friendship with her due to her online presence, but she was a huge advocate for bringing more diversity into paleontology. Being a Black woman in the field was hard, and she was fighting to carve an easier pathway for future fossil nerds like her.

Her smile was like a spotlight, and I felt the hurt from earlier slip a little bit. I accepted her hug immediately and let myself take a breath.

"Blaise!" she sang happily. "I'm so happy I get to finally meet you! You're so *cute*!" She pulled back and look me over. "Oh, I love that scarf. Killing it, babe. Your posts lately have been amazing! The interview you did at the Drumheller site was fantastic. And can we talk about that crazy-ass trailer thing you posted?"

"Thank you, lovely. It's a long story." I motioned behind me towards the doors. "The fair is popping. I really love that idea." I laughed as she dusted her shoulders off.

"Thanks. That was my idea." She shrugged. "Once again, I show my greatness."

"And so modest," I teased, and she winked at me before letting her eyes float to Royal.

"Well, hello there," she purred, holding out her hand. "Who's this?"

"This is my...friend. Royal." The pause that shook the world. I hated how bad it sounded, but it didn't seem to trip either of them up. Royal took her hand and shook it, his smirk already sliding into place.

"Nice to meet you," Royal practically purred back. I wanted to punch him for completely unrelated reasons to being jealous. "Love the dress."

Laila batted her pretty, long lashes at him and smoothed down her devastatingly pretty fossil dress. "Alright, you've buttered me up plenty. You guys wanted to see the fossil prep lab, right?"

"If you have the time," Royal hedged. "We're looking into a series of fossil vandalisms across Canada." He took out his phone and flipped through some screens before showing Laila the screenshot from the security footage he was able to steal. "Does this guy look familiar?"

Laila squinted at it and tilted her head to the side. "We get a lot of people through here but..." She lifted her finger as her face brightened. "Is he Columbian or..."

"Argentinian?" I supplied, and she snapped her fingers.

"Yes! I think that's...oh, hell. What was his name? Roy? Raph? Started with an 'R.'" He came through a couple weeks ago saying he dealt in fossil collecting and wanted to see if we could authenticate his pieces. I showed him around the fossil lab." She lowered her voice a bit and added, "Man was fine as hell."

"We think this guy might be involved in the vandalism." Royal winced. "Was he alone in the lab at all?"

"Shit. Seriously? Yeah, I had to step out to handle an issue and let him look around." She turned and waved for us to follow as she started briskly walking towards the lab. "I swear to God, if he ruined anything important, I'm taking his balls."

Royal and I exchanged looks at the ferocity with which she spoke. I was fairly sure she was not only serious, but had the means to do said act with one motion. It was good to remain on Laila's good side.

Walking into the fossil prep lab was like being in a candy store that smelled like plaster and dirt. Bones were laid out in tables, dirt and dust haloed around them being meticulously excavated. I saw a collection of spinal bones, a large femur, I think maybe an upper maxilla.

It was heaven.

I would have swooned if we weren't worried about R-something fucking up a fossil. Laila began pulling out specimen drawers and checking the contents, moving with rapid succession from one to another.

"Start checking those." She commanded Royal towards a case to the right. "They have some wastebasket taxon we wouldn't have noticed had been tampered with. Blaise, you check the marine bones."

I got to work, opening drawers like I was uncovering the holy grail over and over again. Each one held something unique, and even though I couldn't identify most things I saw, it was still thrilling to see. To work in a place like this, surrounded by ancient life, being on the ground floor for new discoveries and classifications would have been an absolute dream. It would never be my life, but God, I wanted it so bad I could taste it.

I don't know how long we were digging before Laila cursed and slapped the side of a cabinet.

"I found it," she growled, rubbing her hand over her forehead. "Asshole sliced into an ankylosaur dermal plate. What a piece of shit!"

The drawer of mysterious shells and teeth I was ogling was slid shut, and I dashed over to her. Sure enough, a perfect rectangle was sheared out of a beautiful plate, marring the surface of an ideal specimen.

"It matches with what we've seen." Royal shook his head. "Son of a bitch. Do you remember anything else about him? Did he leave a phone number?"

"He did." She exhaled. "I have his card in the office."

"Any cameras?" Royal glanced around the room, and she shook her head.

"No. We never thought someone would come in here and mess up fossils. I feel like such an idiot. We're getting cameras installed now, you can bet on that." She slammed the drawer shut and took a long breath. "This day was so nice until this."

"Sorry we stomped on the good day, Laila," I said gently. "This isn't your fault. Why would you ever think someone would do this?"

"Doesn't bring the fossil back." She sounded so damn defeated. If I didn't hate this asshole before, I sure as hell did now. Seeing my sweet friend so heartbroken made me wish truly violent things to happen to R-something's genitals.

"Knowing his name starts with an 'R' is helpful," Royal offered. "Helps me narrow down names when I get possible leads. This sucks, I know it does, but don't let it ruin the day." He gestured towards me. "B wanted to interview you for his social media account and has been looking forward to it all day. We can get some shots of the carnival too. People will love that."

"Yeah," I agreed. "Babe, we can't do anything about this now, but we can still show off your pretty face and badass carnival. Plus, I really want to play with some bones, and I can't do that if you're sad and violent."

Laila snorted. "Never play with bones angry. That's rule one."

"Unless he's into that," Royal added, and she swatted his chest.

"You." She aimed a finger at him. "I'm watching you."

Royal smirked, and I wanted to fucking die. Laila took a long inhale and smoothed her hair down around her temples.

"Okay, Blaise. Where should we start?"

"Your favorite exhibit first. Then we'll go from there."

"While y'all do that, I'm going to go grab some food. Laila, have you eaten?" Royal asked.

"Not yet. If you wanna be a doll and grab me some pizza from the cafe, I'd owe you my soul. Lunch is on me, by the way. You guys can get what you want."

I told Royal to get me the same, and he peeled off to grab food, while Laila and I walked towards the dinosaur hall. Once he was far enough out of earshot, she squeezed my arm.

"Ooo, Blaise. Tell me about *him*. Royal. Boy, he can be my king."

I laughed but had a hard time knowing what to say. Her very knowing look sliced through me.

"You like him."

"He's a friend," I whined. "Just a friend. A really...attractive friend, but it's not like that."

"You sure?" She raised an eyebrow. "You sure-sure? Because I want to give him my number, but I'm not going to step into something you're tied up in, Blaise."

"He's from Texas, so he's not sticking around once this is over." I shrugged, the effort of doing so draining me. "I just can't do another fling. I'm so sick of them."

"Even with him?" Her eyes went wide. Then she gave my arm a pat. "Okay, I understand. So, if I pass along my number, you won't secretly hate me?"

"How could I possibly hate you?" I was able to pull my lips

into a smile as she leaned against me, looping her arm with mine.

"It's impossible."

The dull ache in my chest from earlier started to ease as we started touring the museum. Laila was a fantastic distraction, full of jokes and wild stories of field excavations gone wrong, insane museum guests, and drinking games with paleontologists. The interview she gave had to be reshot twice because we kept laughing, or she'd pop off with something a little too blue for her professional persona.

It was just what I needed to have a pleasant afternoon.

Royal hung back after he dropped off lunch. He assisted with pictures when needed, but for the most part, he gave us space. Guilt crawled up my spine, knowing he was likely withdrawing because of my reaction to the kiss. Before that moment, he'd been my shadow at the carnival, and I knew he probably wanted to talk with Laila more.

I should have invited him to be part of the interviews and tour. I know I should have.

But I needed air. To keep my head clear for a while.

I wrapped up the last recording we needed while the carnival outside was starting to wind down. Laila had stepped off to talk with her boss while I got some of the videos uploading, and when she appeared back at my side with a big grin, I paused.

"What?" I couldn't hide the wariness in my voice. Was it good news, or was she about to tell me my fly had been down the whole day?

"So, I was just telling my boss about you," she sang, hooking her arm with mine.

The video I was uploading could wait. I stuck my phone in my back pocket. "Yeah?"

"Mmhm. He loves what you're doing with the interviews

and noticed the traction you're getting. I sort of not subtly hinted that you're currently freelancing, but would maybe want a job here." She crunched her nose up. "I didn't misread that, right? Would you want to work here?"

"Yes!" I practically screeched, then composed myself and tried to sound more professional. "Hell fucking yes."

"I can't guarantee anything, but keep in touch." She winked. "I usually get my way when I push hard enough."

"I would owe you my soul, Laila."

"You did the hard work, babe. I'm just making sure everyone else sees it."

I practically floated the rest of the time we were there. Somehow, my ghostly body found Royal, gave Laila a bone-crushing hug, and we migrated back to Dolores.

By the time it was all said and done, we left the museum closer to dinnertime. The pizza we had hours previously had worn off, and I was exhausted from bouncing around the museum all day recording Laila. We left with high spirits, and for a little while, I thought maybe we could just let the kiss from earlier be forgotten.

I was wrong, of course.

"So." Royal held up a card as he climbed into the passenger side of Dolores. "Got R-something's card. It says Ruben Garcia. I doubt it's a real name, but it's better than nothing." He paused, then cleared his throat. "I also got Laila's card. Specifically her phone number."

"Lucky you." I cranked the engine and tapped on my phone, my eyes glued to the screen while I searched for a hotel. "Laila's an awesome person. You'd have fun with her."

"Blaise."

"There's a Hilton not far from here. We can crash there tonight and get a fresh start in the morning." I tapped the navigation and buckled up. "Do you want to grab something to eat on the way?"

There was a long pause, but I refused to look in his direction. It was cowardly, I knew. But I couldn't handle seeing whatever was in his eyes just then.

"Sure," he said after a while, and I pulled onto the road.

The drive was awkward and quiet. No music played. Each little bump in the road announced how rusty and frail Dolores was with the amount of squeaking she did. It only took us ten minutes to get fast food and find the hotel, but Jesus Christ it felt like closer to eternity.

"I'll go get the room." Royal put away his half-eaten dinner and climbed out, and I finally forced myself to speak.

"I think I should get my own room from now on."

I didn't look up from my nuggets, but I knew he was staring at me from the open passenger door.

"Blaise. I'm..." He exhaled, his voice soft. "I'm sorry I crossed the line earlier. You told me that you didn't want us to go there, and I should have respected that."

Dolores dipped as he climbed back inside and shut the door. Somehow, I summoned the courage to look at him, and I was so damn relieved to see that he wasn't annoyed or bored.

He looked...sad. Which made it hurt.

"If you really want your own room, that's fine. I get it. But I swear I'm not going to make a pass at you again. Message received. I'd really like to go back to being your friend if I haven't fucked that up."

I exhaled. "Royal, I don't have it in me to make this complicated. My entire romantic life has been me getting too involved and having someone leave. You get that, right?"

His eyes shifted away from me, sweeping down to his lap. "Yeah."

"You're not staying here after we find these assholes, right?"

He shook his head. "No."

"Then we can't happen." The knot in my chest twisted, driving sharp thorns into the meaty parts of my heart. "We can never happen."

His throat bobbed. "Okay."

Silence fell over us as I leaned back in my seat. The lights of the hotel seemed yellow. Bugs flew near them. One of the letters on the sigh flickered.

It shouldn't hurt this damn much.

God, it did though. It felt like a little piece of me was dying.

Royal cleared his throat in the silence. It was the only noise beyond the cars passing on the highway. "I'll go get our rooms."

I nodded, but he didn't look in my direction before he slid from the van. Watching him walk away under the pale yellow lights felt like I was getting a preview of the future. If it felt like there was a vice around my heart now, it was going to kill me when he left for good.

But only if I let it. This wasn't the first time I'd had my heart stomped all over.

Chin up. Deep breaths. There were much, much bigger things happening beyond me feeling sorry for myself. I could mourn Royal later. Right now, we needed to focus on finding R-whatever and the long-lost Albertosaurus.

What I didn't know was that we weren't doing the chasing.

The strapping herbivore and his cute human companion were in fact being hunted.

CHAPTER ELEVEN

ROYAL

Ruben was a shockingly common name.

With all the miracles the internet can perform, narrowing down information based purely off of the name "Ruben" was damn difficult. Of course the last name was fake. Hell, the first name might have been bullshit too, but I'd rather call him that than Asshole Theropod.

You know what? No, I wouldn't.

Asshole Theropod McFuckface was an elusive prick. Each small thread I found blew away. Each whisper of a lead disappeared. It was like the man was a ghost. I had a couple partials on his face from traffic cameras across the globe, but most of them traced back to men clearly not him for various reasons. Luckily, I had a couple aces up my sleeve, and I wasn't ready to give up just yet.

There was something staring me in the face I just didn't see yet. In my gut, I knew I was close to finding the direction I needed. Since we didn't have anything else solid besides the Canadian fossil trail, we stuck with that.

Things with Blaise got less uncomfortable. Slowly.

His body language screamed how closed off he became,

even if he stayed friendly. He didn't change around me anymore. Didn't flirt, even playfully. I didn't even get a side eye or a lash batting to save my life.

It's like he tossed up a glass wall between us. I could still see him, but I couldn't get close. And damn if the glass didn't get foggy at times.

I'd been around a long time as a human, and I'd had my smatterings of romance. Back in the late 90's, I thought I fell madly in love with both Winona Ryder and Leonardo DiCaprio in the same year. That was a rough fucking summer trying to figure out how to wrangle them into a beautiful interspecies polygamous relationship.

I had charts.

I didn't know what I had now. Did it count as heartbreak if it was never really a relationship? Hooking up in a club wasn't exactly the wild romance we'd tell our future adopted dogs. Well, hypothetical adopted dogs since *we could never happen.*

Fuck. This was the kind of stuff that made Adele such a good singer. I'd have enough melancholy heartache to write a couple albums. The hundred-pound, dinosaur-enthusiast twink crushed my heart.

Write a song about that.

"What's the next stop?" Blaise asked around a bite of Twizzlers.

"Winnipeg. We're heading to the Manitoba Museum next." I plucked one of the long, red licorice sticks from the pack after he offered it to me. "How are your interviews doing on your platform?"

"Amazing. Laila is so damn charismatic and cute. Everyone loves her. Remind me next time to darken my green eye shadow before we go live. It faded, and I just looked like I had bruises or like...an eye fungus. I looked gross."

I snickered. "That can be your shtick."

"My *shtick* is to look cute, not diseased. No more candy for you."

"Brat." My phone vibrated with a new alert from the facial recognition software I had been running. The downloaded photos of possible leads grabbed my attention, and I started flipping through them carefully. A couple were easily dismissed, but there was one that caught my eye.

From downtown Toronto.

Yesterday.

"What the fuck is this guy's problem?" Blaise's annoyed tone pulled me from my focus. He was glaring at his rearview mirror, both hands on the wheel. "Go *around*, asshole truck. Guy is so far up my ass he should be buying me dinner."

The massive truck was so close to Dolores's bumper I couldn't see the grill. It was a muscle machine used for hauling heavy loads, with two back tires and a wide bed, but was driving like it was a little sports car that could whip around cars on a dime. At least, that's what I thought. I assumed it was a frustrated, monumental jerk who didn't like Dolores's speed.

Until it slammed into us.

Blaise yelped and gripped the wheel, righting the wheels as the boxy van teetered and wobbled from the impact. I couldn't see much from the side mirrors other than the shine of the black truck, and Dolores was so filled with Blaise's stuff that looking through the back windows was impossible.

"What the fuck is he doing?" Blaise tried to change lanes, but the truck followed, revving its engine and smacking into us again.

"Pull over, B!" I gripped the handle above the window. "He's going to make us crash otherwise!"

"Are you insane!?" Blaise tried to speed up, but the truck matched us easily. "If he's this aggressive, don't you think he's probably got a gun or something?"

"A gun I can handle. A fiery car cash I can't. Pull over!"

"Handle a gun with what? Your biceps?!" He dodged another blow but nearly lost control of the van in the process.

"Blaise, pull over before we flip!"

"Fine!" He tried to move to the side, but the truck clipped us just right, sending Dolores spinning across the road. We both screamed and clutched what we could as the world around us carouseled, the smell of burning rubber and gasoline assaulting our senses.

By pure luck and maybe some deity I wasn't familiar with, we didn't flip. Dolores whipped across the highway like a metal tornado and slid into the dirt, kicking up a cloud of dust and debris. The sounds of popping metal and settling dirt fogged over us, Blaise's rapid, sawing breath punching through the noise.

"Get down and stay hidden," I commanded, reaching over to shake his shoulder when he didn't respond. "Blaise. Did you hear me?"

His wide, panicked eyes locked on me. "What?"

Movement in the mirrors sent me into action. Two men were walking towards us quickly, splitting in opposite directions to flank each side of the van.

"Get down. Stay hidden," I said again. "Don't come out until I say."

"Fuck." Blaise sank down in his seat and slithered out of it, crawling into the back. I heard him shoving boxes and cases, but my eyes were locked on the guy approaching my side. The matte black gun in his hand was clear as day, even if he was trying to keep it hidden at his side from any potential passing traffic. I'd need to move fast. Very fast.

As soon as he reached to open my door with his free hand, I kicked it open and swung out, jabbing my fist into his throat to send him reeling back. He gagged and choked, raising his arm to shoot blindly, getting one shot off as I slammed his wrist into the side of Dolores. His bones twisted and snapped in my grip. The gun clattered to the ground during the painful scream he let loose.

His nose crumpled when I slammed my skull into it, and I let him drop, grabbing the gun and pulling a bullet into the chamber.

"Don't fucking move!" the other guy shouted, rounding the front of the van with his pistol aimed at me. I aimed my stolen weapon at the guy on the ground.

"I don't like dudes aiming guns at me, man. Tends to piss me off," I warned.

"Drop the damn gun!" he tried again, adjusting his fingers around his weapon. "This doesn't have to get ugly."

I had a perfect zinger lined up about how it had already gotten ugly the moment I saw his face, but Blaise stole my timing. In a blur of faded green hair dye and flashy scarf, the genderqueer force of nature cracked gunman number two over the head with a tire iron. The guy ducked down with a holler, covering his head and toppling to the side, dazed.

I tried to rush in heroically, but Blaise was on him like a pissed-off hornet. He buzzed around him swinging the iron, landing a couple nasty blows on the guy's ribs and thighs.

"Look at my car, you asshole!" Blaise screeched, wailing on the crumpled would-be assassin. "I swear to *God* if you destroyed my wigs, I'm going to rip off your balls!"

"Easy, tiger." I looped my arms around his waist and pulled him back, barely dodging his swinging melee weapon. "We need him alive if we want him to answer questions."

Blaise huffed, pointing his iron at the man I had dealt with. "We already have one alive. I'm killing the driver."

"Let's see which one is the most cooperative." I plucked the gun from the crumpled man Blaise had knocked nearly unconscious and tucked it into my waistband. "Watch him a second."

Blaise panted, his hazel eyes on fire with anger as he glared at the bruised and beaten attacker. The other guy whose nose I had broken whined as I dragged him over by the leg, dropping him beside his aching friend.

"Alright, dipshits. Start talking, or I'm going to let B treat you like meaty piñatas."

"I'll keep hitting you until *something* falls out," Blaise growled, and I whistled.

"Dark."

The guy with the broken nose spit some blood out of his mouth. "Fuck you."

"Your buddy isn't looking great, man," I pointed out, wincing at his friend still holding his head. "I'm pretty sure Danger Twink over here gave him a concussion."

"You're up next if you don't start talking. I'm ready to cave in your skull for what you did to Dolores." Blaise spun the iron in his hand.

"Who?" The guy raised a brow, a condescending tilt to his voice.

"My fucking car!" Blaise took a step towards him, and I put my hand to his chest to stop him. I held back a snicker as Busted Nose flinched.

"Okay, Jesus." He eased himself up to sitting and eyed Blaise warily. "We came to take him to a drop-off location in Ontario." He nodded to me. "And to take your phone," he added towards Blaise. "We were told to rough you up a bit too. Kill you if we had to."

"My phone? Why?" Blaise blinked. "You were going to kill me over my phone?"

"We get paid not to ask questions. I don't know who has

such strong opinions about your phone or your boyfriend, but those were my orders."

"He's not my boyfriend," Blaise said quickly as I mumbled something similar.

The guy looked between us, unamused and bloody. "That's what you're focusing on?"

"Where were you going to take me, exactly?" I asked, pulling my serious tone back into place.

"Gas station outside of Sudbury. We were meeting up with a guy named Kelly for the drop-off." Busted Nose winced as he touched his tender face. "That's all I know."

The guy beside him moaned clutching his ribs. "I might puke."

"Who hired you?" Blaise demanded with a snarl.

"We don't get names." Busted Nose sounded annoyed and bruised. "Just instructions and drop-off times."

"Get up," I instructed with a sigh, keeping one of the guns in my hand. Busted Nose got to his feet, hauling his hunched friend up by the arm. "Get the fuck out of here. We will *not* see you again, clear?"

"You're letting them *go*?" Blaise snapped. "After what they did?"

"They don't know anything, B." I glanced up the road. "Plus if someone drives by, we're all in trouble." I lifted my chin towards their truck. "Get lost. Double time."

Blaise huffed through his nose, glaring at the broken goons that tried to kill us as they limped away. He didn't stop glaring until the truck was far out of sight. Then he erupted into a storm of curses and flailing arms. I'd never heard the combinations of words this man threaded together during his furious meltdown, and I was millions of years old.

He screamed at God, fate, I think Shia LeBeouf, and demanded that the universe repay him for his absolute shitty luck. I gave him a moment to catch his breath before I dared to break the bad news.

I also made sure to remove the tire iron from his hand before I spoke.

"B. I'm going to need your phone."

BLAISE

As if being homeless, jobless, and heartbroken wasn't enough, I had to get my van/house smashed in by two dickless shit weasels.

Who were trying to *kill me* and *kidnap Royal.*

My brain had been firing on adrenaline-soaked rage mode during most of the encounter, and that energy wasn't fading as I tried to pry open the back of Dolores. Her back doors were bent and scraped, paint torn away with streaks of chrome and black marring the surface. The lock was busted, the handle barely functioning as I ripped open one door to see the damage to my life stored inside.

My wig cases were in disarray. My costume trunk was on its side. The guitar I never learned to play but would someday was flipped and almost in the passenger seat. It was a fucking disaster. As I started trying to pull things from the van, Royal took the iron I was holding so I could use both hands.

He may as well have hit me with it with what followed.

"B. I'm going to need your phone."

"Why?" I set a wig case down, staring at him from over my shoulder.

"Because I think they're tracking us through it."

"What?" I scoffed, actually scoffed at this guy, and shook my head. "How the hell would they be doing that?"

"Well, if it was me," he started patiently. "I would have tracked the source of that video you posted—"

"No." I pointed at him. "This is *not* my fault!"

"B," he tried, but I turned on him. It was misplaced and not fair, but Royal stepped into the eye of the storm. I was hurt, angry, my car was screwed up, and my head was pounding.

"How do we know it wasn't you? You do shady, weird computer shit all the time on the deep web, right? Yeah, exactly. You probably clicked on some crazy shit and led them right to us. Look at Dolores, Royal! What am I going to do now?"

"We," he said calmly, putting both of his large hands on my shoulders, "are going to figure it out. Together. Hey." He leaned down to look at me. Big, brown eyes washed over me like a soothing balm. "I'm not going to leave you hanging. And I'm going to help you get Dolores fixed. You have my word on that."

My body shook as I exhaled. "Do you really think it was the damn video?"

"The only people who would care about the validity of that video is my team and whoever that Giganotosaurus was. My guys don't send hitmen to steal phones. They send me and I digitally assassinate data. Or they send a Yutyrannus." Royal shrugged. "You wanted views. You got them."

"They were going to kill me." Saying it out loud made my knees weak. "They were going to kill me, Royal."

"Like hell I would have let that happen, B." The seriousness in his voice weakened my knees more, but for different reasons. The smirk he tossed me after made me lean on Dolores's busted door for strength. "Though you didn't need my help. You beat that man's ass."

"He fucked with my car and my wigs. He's lucky you stopped me."

"Hell hath no fury than when someone messes with Blaise." He held out his hand. "You gotta give me your phone."

"This is my *life*, Royal, and I don't mean it like a spoiled teenager. I mean this is my work, my résumé. I *need* this."

"I know." Royal flexed his fingers.

Anxiety was prison-shanking me in the kidneys as I fished my phone from my pocket. "You're sure?"

"I wouldn't ask if I wasn't." It felt like tearing off my arm as I placed it in his palm.

"I can't watch." I covered my eyes. "Please don't smash it here. I'll die. Go out into the woods and murder it where I can't see."

Royal chuckled. "This isn't the movies, B. I'm not going to smash it."

I peeked around my fingers. "What?"

"I'm going to install a VPN on it so it scrambles your IP. Don't make any calls so you don't ping a cell tower—ow!" He laughed as I slapped his arm. "Why are you hitting me?"

"Why didn't you lead with that! I thought you were going to destroy my phone, you asshole!"

"You just need a VPN!"

"Then why do they break phones in shows and stuff?"

He shrugged. "Dramatic effect?"

"Can't they like...track the...GPS or something?" I motioned towards my phone like it was diseased.

"Not if you turn it off."

"This is stupid." I crossed my arms over my chest, my head aching from my own screaming.

"Would you rather I smash your iPhone?" His brow popped up. "Cause I can if you want."

"I want to get out of here and maybe stab something." I slammed Dolores's warped door twice because the first time it swung open again. "My poor van."

"You think she'll limp to the next stop?" Royal tapped away on my phone. "Or should I call a tow?"

"She'll make it." I gave her a pat. "She's a strong van. She's held together by my love and our mutual tenacity. It's going to take a lot more than a strong ram in the ass to—" I jerked as one of her back tires blew, a hubcap spiraling off across the street. Royal and I watched it roll lazily to the other side before circling melodramatically into the dirt. Then the back door swung open again.

And the bumper fell off.

That's when I cried.

CHAPTER TWELVE

ROYAL

It had not been the best afternoon.

The tow truck took an hour to get to us. Blaise sobbed most of the time we waited. He cried harder when I told him he couldn't do interviews anymore. I didn't have the heart to tell him about the face the mechanic made when I asked what it would cost to get Dolores back up and running. The guy basically told me that my request was pointless without actually saying it, but that wasn't a conversation to have with Blaise right then.

Dealing with a brief encounter with death, beating someone with a tire iron, and learning that he was being hunted by dinosaur shifters was enough for one day. The death of Dolores could wait.

Blaise refused to leave his belongings in the machine's shop, so I was the sucker that played pack mule for his many, many cases. Guilt and my own stupid feelings for the man had me doing things my pride would otherwise had denied. Three wig cases, a costume chest, and a box of shoes was hauled into the hotel room courtesy of Royal Dumbass Bell Service while Blaise was in charge of our regular bags.

I made him leave the damn guitar.

Blaise let our bags drop to the floor and crawled into the bed, laying practically face down in the pillows. I sat by his feet after placing his heavy-as-hell cases down.

"Hey. We're going to be okay, B."

"Let me mourn," he groaned into the pillow.

I gave his leg a pat and stood, letting him mourn while I prepared to break the news to Montana. As if being in Europe wasn't bad enough, now he was going to have to learn someone was chasing me—well, *us,* but I was keeping that to myself at the moment—and aimed to have me kidnapped. If the roles were reversed, I know I'd be stressed as hell knowing I couldn't help one of my brothers if they were in danger.

Hell, I lived through this twice now with Dalton and Baha. Dalton was kidnapped by the cartel, and Baha was trapped on a cruise ship while I was stuck back in Dallas. Sure, my tech skills helped in both situations, but if I could have teleported there to kick some ass, I would have.

The hotel hallway was eerily quiet as I walked down the small flight of stairs outside, which was almost as silent. The nearest hotel to the car shop was a small little blip, surrounded by lush forest that flanked both sides of the road. Next door was a closed donut shop and an empty building for rent. Beyond that, it was just the beautiful Canadian countryside and my bone-deep dread.

That foreboding sense of unease was cranked up to eleven when Montana's number flashed over my screen.

For a moment, I thought about hurling my phone into the abyss as to not face whatever was on the other side. Then I remembered Montana telling me how grounded and patient I was before the mission started, so I cussed, kicked at the dirt, and cursed the universe before answering.

Maybe it was a status check. Maybe he was calling to let me know he was almost here, and I'd have some backup.

Maybe the next time I shifted, I'd grow wings.

Not likely.

"Hey, boss."

"Royal."

Crap. That was mad Montana tone.

"Yeah?"

"Tell me about this livestream on social media and why it's still up." Beyond his angry voice, I could hear the soft rush of traffic from his open window. Distant car horns howled in the background, and I absently wondered where he was.

"I've explained before. Once something is out on the web, you can't really kill it. Re-posts, downloads ,and shares make it like a bad virus, man. You have to snuff it out before it gets out, or it's a Pandora's box situation." I leaned my shoulder against the pillar outside of the room. The paint was peeling and fell away from my touch.

"You've stomped out video from Baha's shift on the cruise," he countered, and I was already shaking my head.

"I had that boat locked down way in advance. This was someone in the wild, not a contained parameter. It's like comparing a bonfire with a forest fire. I've been manipulating the algorithms to make sure it's harder to find, but that's all I can really do. But Montana, no one thinks that video is real. It's mostly blurry and insane as it is."

The long pause on the other end made my stomach tighten. When he spoke again, his voice was a low threatening growl. "Who uploaded it?"

My fingers rubbed along my jaw, my mind floating away with the thought of shaving for a moment. Clearing my throat, I said, "Guy's name is Blaise Fite. He was sneaking onto the site that night and saw us."

"Has he been dealt with?"

"Dealt with?" I pulled my phone back and looked at it like it bit me. "Phrasing, Montana. C'mon, man. I've told you about surveillance. That sounds so dark."

"Calgary, you know what I mean."

Oh, he busted out the codename. He was serious.

"If you're asking if I met him or interacted with him, yes." I couldn't help but glance back towards the room. Jesus, what a mess. *Met* and *interacted* was a hell of an understatement. "He's not a threat."

"Yes he is. Anyone outside of our team who saw what he did is a threat, Royal. This is rule one."

"Can I counter-argue this point? I'm not disagreeing with you, boss. I'm not. But let me say my piece? Please?" I waited, listening to him wrestle between wanting to pull rank and being a brother. Montana was the best at both, but at this point, I wasn't sure which would win over.

"Your piece better be very fast."

By the skin of my damn teeth.

"Remember what I said about getting ahead of information? Once it's out, it's wild and alive. It spreads, it mutates, and it's impossible to kill. Keeping the source of the information close helps control what's released. Blaise has been with me for days, boss. What's he been doing instead of fanning the flames?"

"He's *with* you?" Montana snapped, but I pressed my point.

"Look at his feed. He's been interviewing paleontologists. Gushing about fossils. Being a normal dinosaur geek like Simon. What he's *not* doing is spinning the wheels on the livestream and making it worse."

The poor pillar I was leaning on was damn near stripped of peeling paint I had been nervously picking on. Was that the only reason I had invited Blaise with me on this insane mission?

Hell no. Was I about to tell my leader, a T.rex, that I had a crush on our information leak?

I thought I'd rather swan dive off a cliff, thank you very much.

The long pauses Montana took before answering me drove my anxiety through the ozone, but I didn't dare prod. I waited, ripping dry paint off a pillar, and hoped he wasn't about to rip me a new cloaca.

"How much does he know, Royal?"

Craaaaaaap.

"He saw us shift, boss. I told him a little bit just to keep him from freaking out." It was a lie. I told Blaise everything because post-adrenaline crashes paired with injuries made me a chatty bitch, apparently.

Montana's long sigh was the exact sound I imagine someone's soul sounded like when it was too tired to stay tethered to a body.

"This situation is rapidly getting out of control. I think you need to cut Blaise lose, Royal. Take his phone and drop him off somewhere."

"I can't." I pushed my palm into my eye and pressed down to see the stars.

"Why?"

Oh gee. Lemme think. I was a sucker for cute boys with eyeliner? Or how about Blaise was fun, interesting, and I liked him too damn much?

"Someone came after us today, boss. Two men in a SUV tried to run us off the road. Apparently, they were hired to take Blaise out and take me in." I blinked my eyes open as I shook my head. "I can't leave him now. That's like sending him into the wolf's den with a meat necklace."

"Fuck. Where are they now?"

"I took their weapons and put the fear of God in them.

They're not coming back. I dealt with the security compromise, so they won't find us again." A lone car passed by on the road, breaking the silence outside. "Are you still stuck in France?"

"Spain." Montana let out a long sigh. "I'm trying to get out within the next two days."

"How the fuck did you end up in Spain?"

"It's a long, frustrating story, Royal. But I'm trying to get to you. Have you found anything tangible on who these people might be?"

It was my turn to sigh. "Couple partial facial recognitions. I put out some feelers for the fake name and possible aliases. I think I have a lead in Toronto, so that's my next stop. This guy's good at keeping himself under the radar, I'll give him that. But if I know anything about apex predators, you guys tend to get comfortable being untouchable and make a mistake."

"The dead ones do," Montana said in his "king of the jungle" tone.

"This guy's as good as dead the moment I find him. Have you been keeping up with the files I've sent over? The pictures of the fossils he's butchered?"

"I have. There's a reason he's cutting these fossils up the way he has been, Royal. I have no doubt it's the same reason he took the new shifter you found. Why the hell one of us would be doing this is what troubles me. Something is off. Very off."

Everything about this situation was off, from the motive of Asshole Theropod McFuckface to my shit skills at being a friend.

"Yeah," I agreed. "No shit."

"When you find a lead, promise me you won't go without backup. You're going to Toronto next?"

"You don't think I can handle two theropods at once?" I snorted. "In my sleep, boss man. I'm joking," I cut in as I heard him do his frustrated big brother inhale. The one that happened before a Montana-style scolding. "I'm not budging without backup. I'm not Dalton. And yeah, I'm going to Toronto next. They messed up my ride when they ran me off the road, so it'll be a day."

"You have your Dalton-like moments."

"Uh, excuse you, Dalton has Royal-like moments. Who do you think taught him about anarchy, cherry bombs, and hair dye?"

I had been awake a full year before Montana found Dalton, so I had a head start on being a pain in the ass. Dalton learned his charm from me.

Anything he said was a damn lie.

"Keep me updated on your location, and I'll rendezvous as soon as I can."

"You got it." I blinked and looked at the phone, still surprised when he hung up without saying goodbye.

Theropods, man. Rude.

My stomach was growling as I tasted the leaves rustling in the wind. Most of the new species of flora wasn't something I could digest in my other form, but I still craved them. All of my brothers could go hunting and munch on whatever they could capture, while I had to research plants beforehand, or I'd have explosive stomach problems.

Life's never fair for the veggie-saurs.

The stress of the day had the forest calling to me. I wanted to feel the dirt under my feet, the dew of the grass against my hide. The thought of resting in a field watching the sunset through my ceratopsian eyes was extremely tempting. It was remote enough that I could get away with a nice stroll as long as I stayed away from the road.

But I couldn't leave Blaise to mourn alone. He probably needed to eat as much as I did.

Back in the hotel, I realized that sleeping had won out over all other priorities for Blaise. He hadn't moved from where I left him, except he was curled up slightly, his mouth was open, and eyes shut. Poor guy was out cold, his mascara smudged from the hours of tears, greenish-tipped hair wild around his head.

He was a complete mess.

It made me smile.

This small disaster impressed me. I knew he was strong-willed and took no shit, but I had seen him crumble. I had also seen him floor a guy twice his size and try to go back in for seconds. Small and mighty, that was Blaise. A powerful punch of personality in a world of monotony.

Watching him snooze made my chest ache a bit. I wished I could tell him how amazing I thought he was.

It's not really something a friend said this early in a relationship, though. Especially not after the hiccup days before.

I slipped my hoodie off and used it to cover him since he was sleeping on top of the covers. Blaise gave a little snort and curled up tighter. I left to let him sleep.

My stomach was still roaring. My shoulders were tight from the day.

Fuck it.

I skipped going back to my room and went back outside. The evening was starting to pull the sun down, bugs were warming up their act for a night of serenading, and a pale moon was peeking through the veil. I jogged across the empty road to the long stretch of field before the forest line. The grass folded under my boots with soft whispers. The forest floor was dark and smelled like leaves and dirt as I passed through it, hoping it would open up enough to give me room.

The sound of running water caught my attention, and I followed the sound to a small stream, clear and fresh as it rolled over rocks. I couldn't get my clothes off fast enough, tucking them near the base of a tree so I could stretch into my other skin.

God, it felt good to shift.

My vision changed, weakening slightly as my sense of smell exploded. The rush of the forest made me dizzy, swarming my head as I inhaled deeply.

Water, delicious leaves, mud, bugs, deer, a large mammal predator far in the distance, all swirled through my nose like an abstract painting of scents. It was cold on my hide. My horns brushed a tree trunk as I passed it.

Out of habit, I lifted my nose to smell for my herd, but they weren't there. Not the ones from millions of years ago, with my calves and mates, and not the one now with my theropod brothers.

I was alone. For the moment.

The walk through the forest was calming and quiet. My breath puffed out in steam clouds as I searched for something to eat. The logical, human side of me cautioned about what was tasty and what was poison, but my ceratopsian stomach was starting to win over.

For a couple of hours, I roamed, snacking and drinking from the stream, enjoying the night as a bull in a much smaller world. Once an hour, I smelled for my family that wasn't there, reminded myself I was alone, and kept going.

The fourth time I did so, I found someone.

Herd.

Protect.

I lifted up from where I was sitting and started walking, lifting my nose to breathe in where to go. Back up the stream, through the trees, a couple of which creaked against my weight as I squeezed through them, and close to the line leading to the field.

Herd.

Just there. My herd.

I heard a small gasp, my eyes trying to focus in the weak light. Even though I couldn't see him well, I could smell him.

My mate. My herd.

Blaise's footsteps were soft as he came closer, passing through the trees to where I stood. When he was much closer, I could see him better. Wrapped around his small frame was my hoodie, his hair still a wild mane, makeup still smudged on his face. He smelled like me and him combined, and it made me feel soft and warm.

I pressed my beak against him to smell deeper before nudging him closer to me.

Come with me, now. I'll feed you. I found good plants for you.

I was going to be a good bull for my mate.

BLAISE

AFTER THE DAY THAT I HAD, I SHOULD HAVE EXPECTED something else weird to happen.

I woke myself up snoring in a hotel room I didn't fully remember checking into, surrounded by my beat-up suitcases, draped in Royal's hoodie. Royal was nowhere to be found, his room empty and his phone going to voicemail.

Fearing the worst and imagining worse than that, I started my frantic search for him outside. That's when I noticed heavy footprints leading to the end of the road and continuing across the field. Was it strange for someone to go walk in the woods at night? I didn't fucking know. I thought that's strange and abnormal, so I followed them.

Only to stare down a familiar yet still startling Regaliceratops standing in the goddamn woods.

Then the giant bully started shoving me around with his big face, nudging me this way and that, sniffing me like I rolled in flowers before showing up. I finally shoved his nose away from me and stepped back.

"You have to stop. You're going to knock me over. What?" I watched him turn his head towards the woods, then back to me. "Are you asking me to follow you? No!" I pointed at the dark, creepy woods. "That's how horror movies start. I'm not going in there. Plus, I can't see anything."

Royal lifted his head, then his front leg, tapped it with his beak, and then lifted his head again. He did this three times before the lightbulb in my head finally went off.

"You want me to climb on? Oh my God." I stared at him as he nodded. "Seriously?" He shoved me with his nose again. "Okay! This better be worth it because otherwise I'm kicking your ass."

He huffed, which I wasn't sure if it was a laugh or a sigh of annoyance, but I did what he asked. I stepped onto his front leg as he lifted me up to his neck, where I climbed on like the most ungraceful circus performer trying to mount an elephant. His skin was warm dry pebbles under my fingers, his frill even more formidable up close. His spine was a little uncomfortable against my tailbone, and when he walked, it shifted and moved under me. I was terrified of slipping off but also reveling in the fact I was riding a dinosaur.

"I'm pretty sure there's a drawing of me doing this in crayon," I said with a laugh. "I always wanted a pet Triceratops—not that I think you're a pet," I corrected as he huffed again. "But when I was a kid, this was my top goal in life. I wanted this, the ability to fly, and to be part of the X-men. I wanted to be Storm. Hell, I still do."

He didn't respond, but I think that was because of the lack of vocal cords.

Royal carried me through the woods until we came to a stream. The tree line opened up enough to let the night sky peek through, the full moon dropping bits of silver into the water. It was really pretty and seemed almost magical while sitting on a dinosaur.

I slid down after he lifted his arm again, standing near the water as he started pulling branches down with his beak. Thank God I was wearing his hoodie because it was chilly outside. The fabric was just thick enough to keep the cold at bay, but my legs were starting to freeze through the denim. I watched, totally clueless to what was going on, as Royal piled up branches and leaves in front of me.

Then he laid down near the pile, totally proud of himself. His frill was flushed red, his nostrils flaring.

He pushed the pile towards me.

"Oh." I blinked at the sticks and vegetation before me. "That's for me, isn't it? Well, that's...very sweet, Royal. Thank you."

I don't know how, but I swear he looked like he was beaming. Like I had just told him his frill was the best one in the world, and all of his competition was dead.

I wasn't sure what the most surreal part of this interaction was. If it was the fact that I was standing in some random dark woods at night, the fact that I was doing that with a dinosaur, or the fact that said extinct animal was trying to give me a pile of sticks. It was like having to smile and nod at a kid's macaroni art you had no idea what to do with, and you had no idea what the picture was, but you didn't want to crush their spirit.

Silver lining: I did have the opportunity to be around a real-life Regaliceratops without the threat of being eaten or trampled. Now I could appreciate what my life had become and take the excuse to be a full dinosaur geek for a moment.

I walked around the stick pile and ran my hand up Royal's

cheek to his nose horn. His eyes watched me as I felt the cool bone, tracing my fingers down to his warm skin as I walked to his massive side.

"I've always wanted to do this," I admitted as I leaned against his belly with my arms out, smiling as the rise and fall nearly lifted me off my feet. I laughed, even though my eyes were misting from the experience. "This was my favorite part of *Jurassic Park*, seeing the Triceratops." I shut my eyes, listening to his strong heartbeat.

If I was struck dead that moment, I would have died happy.

I got to listen to a dinosaur breathe. Listen to its heartbeat. I got to feel what their skin was like, what they sounded like. I got to ride one like I was living out every single five-year-old dinosaur kid's dream.

And he brought me sticks, which for some reason was hilarious and fulfilling all at once.

My heart was full. My body was floating.

I had to take a breath and remind myself that I wasn't dreaming. I had never been so damn happy before.

Royal's eyes were still warm and brown, even in his dinosaur form. Somehow I knew he'd be smiling if he had the ability. Lifting up from his belly, I walked back to his beak and placed my palm against it.

"There's nothing simple about this, is there?" I swallowed. "No matter what, this is going to be complicated. Maybe I want it to be complicated."

Royal watched me for a long moment, his pupils flexing as he focused on me. He slowly climbed to his feet as his body began to twist and pop. His skin shifted around his body as bones slid under it, his mass shrinking as his skeleton morphed into something bipedal and fleshy, skin darkening and smoothing out before he landed back in his stunning human form.

It was horrifying to watch, and it made me a little queasy, but the end result was worth it.

Naked, strong, hot as fire, and walking up to me with a smirk. He tried to speak, probably say something cute and funny, but my lips were on his too fast. I wrapped my arms around his neck and pulled him into a kiss, hungry and desperate for his contact. He staggered for just a second as I jumped up and wrapped my legs around him, groaning a bit as his wide palms squeezed my ass.

Lips, tongue, and breaths all tangled together as I devoured him, taking everything he would give me in that moment. I never wanted to stop tasting him, his full lips flavored with crisp spring water and earth, his skin burning against me as I held him close. When I finally stopped for a breath, I felt him shiver and swallow.

"Damn," he croaked, easing me down to my feet. "B, I want nothing more than to just fuck you against a tree, but I'm freezing out here."

"You don't show it." I glanced down, and he smirked. "And yeah, we're not having sex in the woods. That's gross. Can you even fit that back into your pants?"

"It can fit into a lot of tight places."

I shivered at that thought and trotted after him as he made his way to his discarded clothing. I'd never seen a horny man get dressed so fast, though navigating the zipper over his excitement was a little tricky.

I could say with absolute certainty the only way to get me to happily march through a dark forest at night was the promise of a naked Royal on the other side. The crunch of the forest floor under us mixed with our childish giggles reminded me of my teenage years. Splashes of youth-like excitement sprinkled with danger made my veins hum, but it was when Royal took my hand to keep me from falling on my face that my heart took off in a gallop.

By the time we got back to the hotel, we were like hormone-drunk teenagers pawing at each other outside of the door. It took so much effort to get the hotel key out of his pocket that I almost demanded we fuck in the hallway so I didn't have to wait anymore.

Royal walked backwards into the room, one hand behind my head, the other flicking on the light as we staggered inside. Our lips crashed together in punctuated moments, pausing only long enough to slip shirts over our heads or glance down at tricky belts. The smell of hotel sheets and Royal's skin was like a drug, crisp cleaner and heady musk all mixed into one.

The smirk hooking his lips as I pushed him backwards onto the bed was sly and dangerous, his heavy body bouncing on the mattress as he tucked his hands behind his head. I had no intentions of making this a quick encounter, not like our time at the club. I wanted to take my time, drink him in slowly and take him for all he was worth.

If I could only have Royal for a little while, I was going to enjoy every damn second of it.

I mounted his hips like a cowboy, swinging one leg over to sit flush against his ridge while I took in the landscape of his body. Umber skin was painted over firm muscles along his chest, and his arms flexed and bounced as he moved. His stomach was toned with just enough fluff to hide the sharp lines. A black line of coarse hair trailed down his navel, tucking under his pink boxer line.

"I didn't get a chance to see all of you last time," I mused, running my hands down his chest before giving each pec a squeeze. "You were all business."

"Could you blame me?" Rich brown eyes poured over me

like hot fudge over a sundae. "The moment I saw you, I couldn't wait to get you alone."

I leaned down to tease a kiss that was just out of reach. "It was the triceratops necklace, wasn't it?"

"It was you," he purred, liquefying my bones with his tone. "The necklace was just the cherry on top."

God, this man was going to kill me.

His lips caught mine, pulling me right back into the earthquake from days ago. My world shifted, my back pressing against the sheets as Royal towered over me.

My neck was peppered with kisses with just the right amount of nipping teeth. Large hands slipped under my shirt and pulled my hips against his at the same time. I was lost in the storm of sensations. The heat of his skin, his mouth, his hands, trailing over my skin was such a stark contrast to the cold sheets under me. Each breath I took was more of him. His skin smelled like forest and salt, the taste of his lips still clinging to mine.

I whined happily as he kissed down my belly and pulled my jeans down my hips, his nails scratching my skin as my briefs were shoved away. Feeling his hot breath on my cock almost did me in, and I gripped the sheets with both hands like the sensation was torture.

"Too much?" He looked up at me, this impossibly gorgeous demigod hovering above my dick.

"Lord yes," I admitted. "But do it anyway."

I was not prepared for Royal's mouth.

One would think that if you'd had your knob gobbed more than once, you know what to expect. The nice warm suction, the hot wet tongue sliding up and down, the softness of someone's lips gliding over your head.

Fuck all that. What I had known as bliss was nothing compared to the complete cock worship I received from Royal. It was the type of toe-curling, mind-melting, electrifying sexual torture one could expect from a being that had been around the block for millions of years. He took me in deep, swallowing around me while his hands squeezed and petted my thighs and ass. His tongue did impossible things from my base all the way to the tip.

He wasn't afraid to push and explore with his fingers and tongue, devouring me like I was the best-tasting thing he had ever had in his mouth. God, I was a mess with each new trick he pulled. I whined and wiggled. My knees kept trying to ride up as my back arched.

There was no playing it cool here. I had lost all sense of self-respect when he was running his lips over my head. Each time I thought I was going to burst, the pressure so intense at the base of my spine I thought the orgasm would fucking kill me, he'd back off enough to let it simmer down again.

He was doing it on purpose, prolonging every second to drive me insane.

It worked. It so fucking worked. I was fairly sure I praised him as Jesus and called him a cock-teasing bastard in the same breath. The earthquake eased as he rose up on his knees, watching me. I was a panting, wet mess in front of him.

"Fuck," he breathed, his eyes hooded and dark with desire. If I didn't know for a fact he was a vegetarian, I could think he was about to eat me alive. He lifted off his heels just enough to pull himself from his jeans, and he was just as big and delicious as I remembered him.

I tried to catch my breath as he watched me laying there, hard and spit-slick from him playing with me. Watching him flip open his wallet for his condom and lube had me tracing my fingertip over the head of my cock, the tender skin hot and over-stimulated. He hummed in approval, rolling the condom on as I teased a finger down my hip to my ass. Using some of the moisture left behind from his tongue, I slid my finger inside just enough to make my cock jump.

I loved that his gaze was locked on me as I played with myself, easing the muscles while giving him a demonstration of how much I wanted him. White teeth raked over his bottom lip. The sounds of my heavy breathing and groans filling the room.

"If you fuck me right now, I'll cum," I promised. My body was wound so tight that his touch would probably snap my cord. Royal's hands gripped my thighs and pulled me close, the searing tip of his cock bouncing against my entrance as he moved. His motions were fluid and strong. The way he handled my body as he started easing inside lit me up from the inside out.

Each one of my nerve endings was alive with stimulation. The sheets between my fingertips were cold and soft, Royal's skin pressing against my thighs molten hot, matching the burning bliss of feeling his massive cock push inside of me. Electrifying pleasure danced over my spine as he pushed, taking his sweet time to let my body wrap around him. I melted under him, openly begging for him for more as I let my head fall back onto the bed.

I didn't care that our neighbors could probably hear us. I didn't care if I was going full porn star in the hotel bed like I was being paid by the word. The stream of dirty talk and sinful noises spilling from me was like a possession, and the sex-starved demon at the wheel was trying to get a sponsored spot on Pornhub.

"You are a dirty little thing," Royal grunted as he pressed further into me, his mountainous weight crushing me in all the best ways. Two pillars of muscle framed my head as he leaned over me, my legs braced over his shoulders. "I love it."

"Good because I can't fucking stop now," I gasped. "Oh my God you're so big."

"Damn right." He grinned, eyes glued to my face as he finally bottomed out inside of me. A zing of pleasure whipped through me like a bolt of lightning as a small wave of pulses sent a little dribble over my belly.

Royal's brows lifted as he watched little drops of cum drip down. "Did you finish?"

"No," I strained through the thunderstorm coursing through my veins. "You're just really big."

"Fuck that's hot," he mumbled, sealing his mouth over mine as he started to roll his hips. I had lost all proper function of myself, so my kiss was mostly just groaning into his mouth. Each jab of him against my insides made me drip a little more, my muscles tight and burning from end to end. It was like I was having mini-orgasms each time he moved, which was short-circuiting my poor brain. My dirty talk turned into pleas, my fingers digging into his meaty shoulders as his skin slapped against mine.

He let my legs drop to his waist as he sat back on his knees, his big hands gripping my hips and lifting my ass up against him. I wish I could say I was able to admire how gorgeous he looked as he fucked me, with his skin shiny with exertion, his big muscles flexing as he moved with precise, targeted movement. But I was so far gone at that point. My body was a current for his electric pulses, my body racing with so much intense contact that all I felt was his dick slamming into me.

I pushed myself up onto my elbows to angle him just right, wrapping my legs tight around him.

"There!" I begged. "Oh fuck, there!"

Brows furrowed as he held me in place, one big hand wrapping around me to squeeze at just the right moment. The fragile thread holding the tidal wave at bay snapped so violently that blasts of light danced behind my eyelids. Hot liquid striped my chest and chin, and I was fairly sure it hit some other spaces as well.

Whoever was in charge of scrubbing the wall behind the bed, I was so sorry.

My arms failed me, and I collapsed to the bed, my body jerking and pulsing as Royal continued to pound into me. I whined at the sensation of my body ebbing down from the high, gasping when he suddenly pulled out.

He hissed through his teeth as he pulled the condom off, jerking himself off over my already soaked stomach and chest. His face twisted in pleasure, his mouth falling open as he moaned. If I hadn't already drained every last bit of satisfaction from my body, I would have cum again from watching his face. A beautiful shiver ran up my spine as he slid our wet cocks together, mixing the moisture between us.

"Damn, Blaise. Goddamn," he breathed. "You're about the sexiest thing I've ever seen."

"Have you not seen yourself?" I cracked my eyes open after they fell shut. "You're like my ultimate wet dream." I dabbed a finger in the sexy mess on my stomach. "Literally."

Royal disappeared into the bathroom, the tap turning on for just a moment before he came back with a warm washcloth for me. I happily accepted it, since the lust-drunk nature of the situation splattered over me was starting to wear off. It had gone from deeply sexy to gross by the time I did the first wipe-down.

"Lord. I need a shower."

"Are you going to take a Blaise marathon shower or a quick after sex shower?" he teased. "Because I would also love a scrub-down."

"Beauty takes time, Royal," I teased back as I got to my feet, smirking as he pulled me over for a kiss. Since we weren't hot and heavy anymore, the kiss was soft and sweet, making a blossom of warmth unfold in my belly.

"You don't need any more time, B. You're gorgeous."

I hummed. "You just don't want me to hog the hot water."

"I really don't like cold showers," he mumbled into my lips. "Please and thank you."

I gave his big chest a pat and disappeared into the bathroom, taking my time to clean up, but cutting my normal routine down to the basics. The things we do for love, right?

Or whatever Royal and I had together, anyways. I wasn't sure if the L-word fit, considering the very real time limit on our time together. Either way, I skipped my normal skin care regimen to make sure he could get cleaned up before bed.

If that's not something of at least strong affection, I don't know what is.

When Royal appeared after his shower, nude and wet, I contemplated trying to go another round. I even tried to give him a flirty look, complete with the classic lower lip bite paired with the "come fuck me eyes." My masterful work was dashed by a jaw-cracking yawn that made him laugh.

"Ditto." He pulled the covers back to join me, when he paused. "This is awkward. Um, is it okay if I stay?"

"Isn't this your room?" I glanced around at the hotel room. "Why would you leave?"

"If you wanted space? I'll go to your room."

I shook my head, giving the bed a pat. "Stay. I kinda fucked up the 'no complications' thing by fucking you. It's complicated now, but I don't want to think about that tonight. I just want you."

He crawled into bed, wrapping his big arms around me like I was the only thing keeping him from floating away.

Royal inhaled slowly, his chest swelling against me. "You know, you never did tell me your first name."

"And I never will," I said around a yawn. My eyes were

starting to droop when the spark of fear made them shoot back open. "Royal."

"Hmmm?" I could hear the smile on his lips.

"Royal," I warned again, angling my head up to glare at him. "You didn't."

"It's really not that bad."

"Ugh." I pressed down into his chest to hide.

"Fredrick is a cute name."

"Freddie Fite is like a B-tier superhero's alter ego. It sounds like his superpower would be that he could turn into a puddle of lukewarm water."

Royal's chest bounced my head as he laughed. "It does not."

"Says the man named *Royal.*"

"I like your name." He smiled down at me. "But I'll call you Blaise if you really hate it."

"I really hate it," I confirmed. "Blaise is mine. Fredrick isn't."

He gave a nod, and I settled back down into his arms again. Warm skin pressed against me from head to toe, the smell of the sharp hotel soap sticking to air between us. His body was like a cocoon around me.

"I hope it doesn't make me an asshole," Royal said softly into my hair. "But I'm kinda glad it's a little complicated now."

My heart squeezed, and I wasn't sure if it was a good tension or not. Either way, I fell asleep thinking the exact same thing and hoping like hell I survived the other side of it.

CHAPTER THIRTEEN

ROYAL

"You wanted to do a drag story time?" I asked around my bite of pancakes. We had ordered breakfast delivery to the room and ended up fooling around before eating it right away, so the food was a little cold. But it was still breakfast food after sex, so it was damn good.

Blaise wore just my hoodie and his briefs and somehow made eating waffles sexy. He dabbed a bit of syrup from his mouth with his tongue and nodded.

"You've seen that in libraries, right? Queens go in and read stories to kids? I wanted to do that but books about dinosaurs and paleontologists to kids. That's, like, dream job goals."

"I love that." I poured a bit more sugary goodness over my cold pancakes. "Have you tried to get a museum or library on board?"

"That's for after I land somewhere, I think. It takes so long to coordinate with a place. Who knows where I'll be when they have an opening. *If* they would ever go for it." He held out his hand for the little packets of syrup. "Any updates about the fossil mutilators? Did your fancy hacking skills pay off yet?"

I passed him the syrup and his phone. "I'm about to go

check. I assume you'll want to check your stuff while I check mine. VPN still in place?"

"Yeees," he whined around his food. "I'm not going to check in or post where we are, either. I do not want a repeat of yesterday. Well." He grinned. "Maybe some of yesterday."

"Or this morning." I leaned in and kissed his sticky-sweet lips before getting up, taking my pancakes with me. My laptop faded to life as I opened it, and I began surfing through my updates. After finding that possible lead in Toronto, I narrowed the search down to that city, gambling on my hunch. It would make sense that they didn't venture out of the country, though hauling a possibly still-shifted theropod through a major city was ballsy.

Honestly, though, most people would just think it was a movie prop or a museum PR stunt to see a sleeping Albertosaurus being lugged around. Toronto was a cool place, and seeing something as bizarre as a snoozing dinosaur would be fun, not terrifying. My sweeps of social media feeds didn't pull up any candid shots of a tarp-covered meat-eater, so either they locked him up in a big truck, or he shifted down before travel.

So, I refocused on Mr. Ruben Asshole McFuckFace and his not-so-ugly mug. It still pissed me off that the guy was handsome. You couldn't be attractive and a fossil thief.

Okay, I guess Jackson would argue that point. As would Baha, since he's all lovey-dovey on the cowboy now.

You know what I mean.

I pulled up the picture that had been caught on the street camera days prior and glared at it. That slightly blurry picture had to be him. I knew he was in Toronto; I just wasn't sure where. It was a big city to start combing through, but being alive for millions of years did give me a buttload of patience. I *would* find this guy and the fresh shifter he kidnapped. And as soon as Montana got here, we'd take the son of a bitch down together.

"Ah!" Blaise shot out of bed, gripping his phone with both hands.

I stood quickly. "What? What happened?"

His hazel eyes were wide, his mouth open in shock. "Oh my God."

"Blaise, *what*?"

"I got the job!" he breathed out in a rush. "I got the job!"

"What job?" I was beyond confused but couldn't help but chuckle as he started bouncing around the room.

"At the Royal Saskatchewan Museum! Laila said her director wants me to come work for them and help with outreach! Holy *shit*!" He slammed into me, hugging me tight. "I can't believe it!"

"Congrats, B!" I wrapped him up with a squeeze. "When do you start?"

"Two weeks." Blaise's cheeks were red from smiling so wide. "I have to figure out what to do about a car, but I'll make it work." He bit his lip and looked up at me, the joy in his eyes faltering slightly. "We still have some time to hunt this thief down together."

"You still want to?" I took his shoulders in my hands. "B, yesterday was intense. I figured you'd want to bow out of this bullshit after that."

An offended look crossed his beautiful features. "And leave you to face these guys alone? Are you kidding?"

"I have backup coming soon. I won't be alone long." I smirked as he shook his head and jabbed a finger into my chest.

"Fuck that. I'm seeing this through. Within two weeks, because after that I have somewhere to be." He flapped his hand dismissively. "So you better speed it up with the computer skills, Mr. Hacker."

The sharp twist in my heart when he leaned against me for another hug almost took my breath away. I loved it as much as it ripped me apart. When I wrapped my arms around him, I felt him holding his breath, and I wanted to exhale for both of us.

My phone rattled against the desk, giving Blaise a reason to slip away and retreat back to the bed. Scooping up my phone, I unlocked it to see a message from Montana sent earlier in the morning.

Montana: Change of plans. Your backup will be there by 10:00.

I flicked my eyes up to the time at the top of my screen. It was ten thirty-five.

I started texting back to ask for details when knocking came from the hotel door. Blaise stood slowly from the bed, his gaze bouncing from me to the front of the room. Worry creased his face, and he grabbed the tire iron from under the bed.

I motioned for him to stay there as I moved to the door, careful not to stand directly in front of it on the off chance it wasn't someone friendly.

"What's the password?"

"Treestar."

Thank God.

I swung the door open with a smile. "My man."

Dalton's crooked grin was almost as wonderful as seeing Blaise's smile. "Someone order a fresh order of kickass?"

BLAISE

I BARELY HAD TIME TO PULL ON SOME PANTS BEFORE ROYAL let the two men inside. Greeting strangers in my underwear never left the best impression, but that was almost how I met Royal's brother and his boyfriend.

"I thought you two were in West Virginia?" Royal followed

Dalton and Simon into the room after locking the door. "How the hell did you two get way up here so fast?"

"Because Dalton drives like a bat out of hell." Simon rubbed at his eyes, clearly exhausted.

"We were in Michigan visiting Dinosaur Gardens." Dalton walked into the room, his pink hair bright and swept back. The shirt he wore had a T.rex trying to grab a magic lamp, his thought bubble showing that he longed for giant, strapping arms. Icy blue eyes landed on me, and he flashed a toothy smile. "Hey, you must be Twizzler guy."

"Is that code?" I glanced towards Royal.

"Guys, this is Blaise." Royal motioned his hands between me and his family. "B, this is Dalton and Simon."

While Dalton was a grinning goof, Simon was a reserved man with a friendly smile. I could see why Dalton was all about him—he was adorable with his graying hair and pretty brown eyes. Plus, he was a paleontologist, so his geeky fossil knowledge gave him twenty hot points to me, as did his tan.

"Hi," I said lamely, bending to tuck the tire iron back under the bed. It was suddenly very obvious to me that I was wearing Royal's hoodie, and I didn't know what to do with that. The grin on Dalton's face made it clear he already knew.

Great.

"Montana mentioned that you may have found a lead on the kidnapper?" Simon glanced around for a place to sit. I mumbled an apology and folded the blankets back over the bed so he could sit. I also dove across the bed to slap a condom wrapper into the trash can and try and pass it off like I was just excited to lay down.

"A partial facial recognition in Toronto." Royal took his seat at the desk, Dalton following to lean an elbow on his shoulder.

"That him?" Dalton whistled. "Kinda hot."

"Not fair, right?" Royal snorted. "I'm hate-crushing on the dude."

"Is he the Giga that chewed on you?" Dalton leaned forward to squint at the screen. "He seems like the type."

"I'm not sure if he's a shifter, but I know he's one of the guys carving up fossils." Royal's fingers flew across the keyboard before he rolled his mouse wheel. "I've been trying to narrow the search around the city for any leads."

"Does that mean we're heading for Toronto next?" Simon asked from where he perched at the edge of the bed. "That's a large haystack to sift through."

"Yeah, but it's the only haystack we have at the moment," Royal sighed. "I've already reached out to the Royal Ontario Museum to see if they'll let us look around."

Simon and I both made happy noises. The dinosaur shifters both looked very amused.

"Is that one of the bucket-list museums?" Dalton smirked at his boyfriend. "You're making the swoony fossil face."

"They have one of the largest fossil collections in Canada," Simon gushed, moving his hands as he spoke. "Do you think they'll let us back into the collections room?"

"Oh my God, can you imagine?" I swooned along with him. "Royal can get us back there. Right?" I leaned forward to look at him past Simon. His smirk was soft around the edges, the fondness in his expression a silent dagger in my heart.

"I bet we can work something out. You know you can view their collection online, right?"

"Really?" I sprang to my feet and trotted over to the desk, leaning over to see his screen.

"I'm working!" he said around a laugh. "Look it up on your phone!"

"I'm not looking at a brilliant fossil collection on my tiny phone when you have a laptop right here." I gestured towards the screen violently. "Go!"

"You are such a brat," Royal mumbled, shrinking one screen before pulling up a new one. After he typed in the address, he turned the screen my way. I snagged the computer and brought it back over for Simon and I to properly fawn over.

"Woooow." Dalton clicked his tongue. "You just got bossed around by a guy, like, a third your size."

Royal just gave a lazy shrug, completely unphased. "Y'all need some time to rest before we hit the road?"

"Dalton hasn't slept in twenty-four hours." Simon didn't glance up from the fossils as he spoke. "He wanted to make it here almost on time."

"I can sleep in the car. Speaking of wheels, do you want to just ride with us, or should we caravan?" Dalton leaned his hip against the desk.

"Well, my van was murdered by some hired fuck-lords who wanted to kill me and kidnap Royal, so I guess we're riding with you. Oh, look at that ichthyosaur!" I pointed at the screen so Simon could click on it.

"Beautiful," Simon agreed with a happy sigh. Then he blinked and looked at me in horror. "Wait, what?"

"Hell yeah, road trip!" Dalton grinned at Royal, his lip piercing catching the light. "Feathers and Frills teaming up again."

"Fangs and Fuckery," Royal added as they went into an unnecessarily complicated handshake that only two million-year-old children could possibly concoct.

"Nerds," I said, scrolling through the online vertebrate fossil collection. The paleontologist sitting next to me chuckled.

CHAPTER FOURTEEN

ROYAL

Loading up Blaise's copious wig and costume cases into the back of Dalton's rented SUV was about ten percent Tetris skills and ninety percent luck. Simon and Dalton had taken up a good portion of real estate with their camping gear, which had to be unloaded and reloaded a good four times.

Once the trunk was successfully closed, we vowed never to open it again.

It was going to take about a day to get to Toronto from where we were, so I offered to drive. Blaise had been behind the wheel during all of the trip so far because he had insisted he was the only one to pilot his beloved Dolores. Dalton had driven for hours to get to us on time, and his road skills were terrifying at best.

I glanced back in the rearview at the sound of snoring. Dalton had his head in Simon's lap in the backseat, one boot sticking out the window as he slept peacefully. Simon's fingers absently ran through Dalton's wilted mohawk while he read a paperback of *The Rise and Fall of the Dinosaurs*.

Blaise was still scrolling through the fossils on my laptop, determined to look at every single specimen they had photos for on the off chance we couldn't get into the museum. At some point he had touched up his eyeliner, the new sharp wings to his cat-eye looking stark against his pale skin. Faded green curls sat a little more behaved today, and my hoodie was wrapped around his small frame like a king-sized blanket.

It made me smile for some reason.

The reason for us being on the trip was treacherous, I had no illusions about that, but damn did I love pretending it was a vacation and not a mission. All of us together, hitting cheesy dinosaur theme parks to let Simon and Blaise rip into the inaccuracies, offended on our behalf, while hitting museums in between? That sounded like the best trip imaginable.

For a fleeting moment, I let myself think, *Maybe we can do this in a couple of months.*

Reality sure could hit like a dump truck.

"Royal?"

Blaise's voice was like a slap back into the moment, breaking my daydream into confetti.

"Yeah?"

He turned my laptop towards me. "You have a notification on another screen."

I glanced briefly. "You can open it. I think that was the search I was running on properties owned by any 'Rubens' in Toronto. Did it land on anything?"

Blaise turned it back towards himself and slid his finger along the computer's trackpad. A smirk curled his lips. "Says there's a building downtown owned by a Ruben Garcia. And looky here. There's a scanned photo of his passport."

I moved my eyes from the road to look at the screen, a bolt of excitement racing up my spine. Staring forward from a grainy copy of a passport photo was the asshole we'd been chasing for days.

"That's him. That's him, B."

"Says that the building," he trailed off as he kept scrolling, "is zoned for food and beverage. Hmm." Blaise started typing, his eyes locked on the screen in concentration.

"Address?"

He grabbed his phone and tapped away before slipping it into the clip-on holder attached to the dash.

"Follow that. I think we found our thieves," he said with a devilish grin. "I brought my tire iron."

"I need you to be seventy percent more April O'Neil and a hundred percent less Raph."

Blaise shrugged. "Why can't I just upgrade to Raph?"

"Baha's Raph," Dalton mumbled against Simon's stomach.

I motioned back towards Dalton's valid point. "And Raph isn't my type."

"Fine." Blaise lifted his nose. "Then I'm a mix of Casey and April. I'm sassy, look good in a jumpsuit, and can wield a weapon."

"Hot," I confirmed.

"What are we talking about?" Simon looked up from his book. "Who's in a jumpsuit?"

Dalton hummed and hugged Simon around the waist, his face nuzzling against his stomach. "I wanna see you in a jumpsuit."

Simon's cheeks flushed, and he went back to his book.

The excitement of the lead made us driven to stay on the road as long as possible. We stopped over night at a small hotel when I couldn't hold my eyes open any longer, and slept a couple of hours before hitting the road again early the next morning. Hours later, we cruised into downtown Toronto to hunt down Asshole McFuckFace.

Even though it had been near ten years since I'd been in downtown Toronto, the bustling jewel of Ontario still captured my imagination. Its unique, glittering skyline was a glass jungle of beauty, alive with concrete veins steaming with people. Fast-paced culture blinked from adverts smiling down from pillars, the smells of gasoline and food tangled in the air.

Damn did I miss Toronto.

Navigating city traffic, no matter where you were, was a test of patience. Being in the tangle of busy roads and side streets made me all the more relieved I was the one driving instead of Dalton. We would have been cruising down a sidewalk within ten minutes if he was behind the wheel. Blaise's phone barked electronic orders at us as we slowly crawled through downtown, inching our way through the city. Eventually, we slid down the street where the building lived.

The strip of bars and clubs were docile at the moment, far too early in the day for the popping nightlife of downtown. Between a few were chain restaurants filling with lunch crowds, but the sleepy bars were getting little love at the moment. Towards the far end, a closed club caught my attention.

"That's gotta be it." I slowed as much as I could without causing a traffic jam so we could peer at the building. Blaise's phone announced we had arrived at our destination as we passed the dark building.

"Jush?" Simon peered out the window. "Is that French?"

Blaise wheezed. "You're so cute."

"Not exactly." I swung into a parking space that opened along the street, secretly praising myself for squeezing the SUV into a metered spot. I snagged my laptop back from Blaise after parking, digging into what I could find out about the club.

A quick search confirmed what I already knew. And Blaise was still cackling.

"Is it a strip club or something?" Simon was obviously confused from the laughing in the front seat and was unfamiliar with the lexicon. "What am I missing?"

"It's a drag club," I said over my shoulder. "With a large

underground basement area they open up for special events and dungeon nights. Damn, looks fun. Looks like they do shows every weekend, and this next one is their annual talent show."

Dalton mumbled something about rabbits and sat up, rubbing his eyes with his knuckles before blinking. "Did we find it?"

Simon pointed out the window, and Dalton half crawled into his lap to peer outside.

"The fossil thieves own a drag club." Blaise shook his head in amazement. "I have no idea what to think of that. Obviously, the Albertosaurus can't be here, right?"

"Where else can they stick him?" I shrugged, looking at the event pictures online. The massive, almost warehouse-style basement under the club was huge enough for a large gathering of bodies to sardine together for a rave or for fun, kinky equipment to be set up. It would be plenty big enough for a theropod to hide, but not a ton of room to stretch their legs. "That basement where they have their big events is pretty damn big and has huge garage doors that open up onto the street around the other side of the club."

"And you think these idiots would risk shoving a dinosaur in there during an event?" Blaise raised his eyebrows, his tone overflowing with cynicism. "What if it gets out? Or roars? Or bangs on the fucking walls?"

"We don't roar," Dalton said around a yawn. "We squawk like badasses."

"It's a valid point," Simon agreed. "That seems beyond reckless."

After what I had seen of Ruben's handiwork in the museum and how diligently he covered his tracks, I knew for sure they weren't wild cards. They were smart. Calculating. And there was something about all of this that sat in my gut like a hot stone.

"I don't think they're idiots or reckless. Logically, this is the only place I could imagine they had to take the Albertosaurus and probably some of the fossil pieces they've been stealing. Maybe they use the noise of the events to hide what they're keeping in the basement." I leaned back in my seat and sighed. "We're going to have to get inside and find out."

"What, now?" Blaise's eyes widened in either fear or excitement.

"No," I laughed. "Tonight. Breaking into a building during the day is how people get shot, B."

"Don't these guys know what you look like, though?" Simon scooted forward between the front seats.

"Easy," I said with a smirk. "We go in disguise."

"Fuck *yes*," Blaise giggled. "I already love this idea."

"I'm not following." Simon glanced between us. "How?"

"Oh shit." Dalton grinned, pressing his shoulder against Simon's as he leaned up to squish between the front seats. "Are we gonna fucking *Birdcage* this?"

Simon's look of confusion drained into horror. "Oh my God."

"If we're going to do this, we need to shop," Blaise piped in immediately. "Wigs I have covered, but I sure as hell don't have outfits for you two." He motioned between me and Dalton. "Dalton has shoulders for days, and Royal is thick with four C's. How are you in heels?" Blaise swiveled in his seat to look at the mixture of emotion beside him.

"Decent." Dalton teetered his hand side to side. "Lower the better."

"Oh my God," Simon said again.

I checked the date on my phone. "It's Thursday. Is that enough time to get something pulled together? If not, we can try for a plan B."

Blaise pinned me with a condescending look of concentrated sass that almost burned a hole through my head.

"Hon-ney. What sort of Queen do you take me for? I'll worry about the details." He swirled his finger to incorporate all of us. "You all start thinking of your personas and names. We have a lot of work to do."

"Have I mentioned how much of a fan I am of you?" I smirked. He tossed imaginary hair back from his shoulder.

"I know."

"Operation Birdcage!" Dalton hooted.

"Oh my *God,*" Simon groaned.

BLAISE

THE HARDEST PART OF PUTTING TOGETHER A PROPER outfit, always, was finding the right shoes.

This was further complicated by the fact that men typically have giant feet, and the styles needed to pull off a proper drag ensemble run small. I can't imagine how difficult it must have been to find men-sized heels before the age of the internet. We were further blessed that Toronto had not only costume shops, fabric stores, and a plethora of makeup boutiques, but also a network of queens who did swaps, sells, and so on. Most of my day consisted of haggling over the internet while picking out sequined fabric and used costume pieces.

It was exhausting and utterly amazing. I also bought another wig, but I kept that to myself.

Royal was my chauffeur while Dalton and Simon rested back in the hotel. He helped me decide between some pieces, carried the bulk of the bags between trips, and sat patiently at the makeup counter while I tracked down the right shade of foundation for him.

He smirked at me while I tested some blush on his cheek. "You're having a blast with this, aren't you?"

"Absolutely." I leaned back, moving his chin from side to side to compare shades. "This is my favorite part of the trip so far."

"Yeah? I guess I need to up my game."

I mirrored his smirk. "Okay. Second favorite."

"Maybe we can make it your third favorite when we get back," he purred, and I nearly dropped my brush.

"Easy, boy. I need to get to sewing if we're going to have something to wrap around you this weekend."

"I know what *I* want wrapped around me."

A shiver ran up my body, and I inhaled, snatching my selections from the counter. "We'll take these. C'mon."

Royal laughed as I tugged him to the checkout line, yelling at the cashiers that I had a family emergency and needed to cut ahead. It didn't work, so I stood in line trying to hide my excitement as Royal grinned like a cocky bastard.

After a pit stop of lunch and a quick fuck in the hotel room, we put on some music and got to work. My sewing machine chugged along while Royal's fingers rhythmically tapped out on the keyboard, hunting down as much information as he could about the club, owners, staff, and so on.

Ruben was the owner of both the building and the business, but he had his name buried behind various alias and business LLCs that Royal had to chip through tons of legalese to track it down. I think only a man with millions of years worth of patience could deal with that much paperwork and data because I took one look at the screen and wanted to rip my hair out.

"So, question." I rethreaded the machine and slipped some

pins in place. "How are we going to get the Albertosaurus out of the club once we find him?"

"That is the ten-million-dollar question," Royal sighed. "My hope is that I can get him to shift down if he isn't already in his human form."

"How?"

"Montana said that we're more keyed into body language in our shifted forms, which makes sense. Even not knowing the species, you can read the basics of animal behavior. All animals, humans included, have tells. Maybe if I go in relaxed and unthreatening, he'll respond to that and feel safe enough to shift down."

I paused my sewing. "Wait. Your plan is to go in there as a human? Are you nuts?"

"If I go in as a big bruiser Regaliceratops, he's going to assume I'm trying to pick a fight. Our species don't have a great history of being nice to each other. Mainly because his kind likes cera-burgers."

"At least when you're in burger form, you have horns!" I gestured towards him. "You're cute, Royal, but you can't take a tyrannosaur in your hot human form."

He leaned back, lacing his fingers behind his head. "I'm not trying to take him. I'm trying to calm him down so he'll go with us willingly."

"And when that doesn't work, what's plan B?"

"Knock him out, load him into the back of a truck with a sign that says 'Please don't feed the dinosaur?'" He shrugged. "I'm open to suggestions."

He grinned as I glared at him. "I thought you were a professional at this?"

"What the fuck gave you that idea?" he asked with a laugh, then pointed to himself. "Guy in the chair, remember?"

I shut my eyes, rubbing at my temples to massage the headache away. "We're so fucked."

"Hey," he called gently, waiting until I looked at him before continuing. "We have safe houses all over the place stocked with supplies. Dalton made a stop on the way up here to grab some supplies, including some powerful sedatives. If shit goes sideways, we have something strong enough to at least bring down the Albertosaurus. We'll be okay."

"What about the Giganotosaurus? Do you have enough for that guy too?" I pulled Royal's hoodie around me, chilled at the memory of steak-knife teeth going into his back. He stood from his desk and tugged me to my feet. Hugs from Royal were beginning to be the only thing in the world that made life seem less catastrophic at times.

The thought of his arms around me being a limited source of comfort made me hold on a little tighter.

"You know I won't let anything bad happen to you, B," he whispered into my temple, his body swaying with me in the middle of the hotel room.

"I'm not worried about me, jackass." I pressed my forehead against his shoulder, shutting my eyes at the feeling of his lips against my hair.

"The odds are much better now that Dalton is here," he assured me, one hand soothing my back with long, gentle strokes.

"A raptor and ceratopsian versus two giant theropods? How is that even?" I tilted my head up as he took my chin between his fingers and lifted. Big brown eyes melted into my gaze, and I felt that warmth all the way through my chest.

"Trust me, Blaise. Dalton and I can handle much bigger than that asshole."

I sighed some of my worries away as he kissed me, the

stubble across his jaw rough against my fingers as I cupped his cheek. "If you say so."

"I do." He kissed me again, long and slow. "Why don't you take a break and I rub your shoulders a bit?"

"Don't threaten me with a good time." I smirked against his lips, stealing one more peck before sitting on the bed. My phone lit up as Royal climbed onto the bed behind me, the weight of him tipping the mattress and scooting me back. Across my screen was a message from Laila, reminding me to send over documents to the office for my hiring paperwork. Attached was a photo of the office space she had made for me next to hers with the caption, "Desk neighbors. Xoxo."

The sparkles of excitement flared and died like the ashes of a dying cigarette. Royal's fingers squeezed into my muscles gently, the knots from my stress pressing back against his strength. The next chapter of my professional life should have been the bright spot just over the horizon. Instead, it felt like a golden weight resting on my chest.

Soon it would be all I had. All I've ever wanted.

I thought moments like this were supposed to feel amazing.

So, why did it hurt so damn much?

CHAPTER FIFTEEN

BLAISE

"It's not that hard. You just tuck and tape."

It's one thing to read instructions on the web, but it's much easier to understand the concept when someone demonstrates. Or that was my reasoning as I walked through the steps of getting my junk streamlined in order to fit into my dress properly. I had anticipated the winced looks of discomfort and the buckets of questions.

I didn't expect Simon to faint.

And I didn't expect Dalton to get it on the first try. Royal took a couple tries, two false victories, and some wasted tape, but he eventually got it down. Or up, rather.

"I can't do it." Simon's eyes lifted from the supplies I put in his hands. "I don't think my body will do that."

"All dicks can do it, Simon. I promise you can."

"Can't I just wear pants or shorts or something?" He swallowed, staring down at the supplies again.

"You most certainly cannot," I scolded. "I spent two days making your outfit. My fingertips are raw, I pricked myself like thirteen times, and I barely slept. Tuck and glam up, Simon Slay. I still need to do your makeup."

Simon swallowed and nodded, giving his boyfriend a worried look before retreating to the bathroom. Dalton followed him, still marveling at his own tape job.

"Wig first or makeup first?" Royal asked, sitting across from me.

"Makeup." I brought my kit over and started priming his skin. "Do the boots fit okay?"

"Mm-hm." He shut his eyes as I dabbed the cream over him. "Not sure about the boobs you got for me, though."

"You were damn lucky a bigger queen was selling her old pair. Otherwise, I was going to be shoving balloons down your dress." I smirked as he laughed. "Did you settle on a name?"

"Royal Majesty. I feel like I can rock that."

"I had a feeling you'd go with royalty as your moniker. I have just the thing for that."

"Oh?" He lifted his brows, apologizing as I reminded him to hold still.

"You'll see later."

"Huzzah!" Dalton announced as they walked out of the bathroom, presenting Simon's hips to us proudly. "Tuck achieved!"

"Dalton." Simon shoved his presenting hands away.

"Good job. Start getting your base makeup on. I'll help once I'm done with Royal."

Simon sat across from Dalton, helping his excited boyfriend get the basic primer and foundation on their faces like it was rocket science. Getting full drag makeup on Royal wasn't as painful as I thought it would be. The only true hiccup we had was gluing the false eyelashes in place, which resulted in him looking like a horror movie villain before it was stripped and corrected.

I muttered more than once how much I'd kill for his full lips. The glitter red on them made him so glamorous I wanted to die with envy and make out with him at the same time. It was all very ambivalent and powerfully gay all at once.

Dalton was a fucking nightmare.

That man couldn't sit still longer than four seconds and practically vibrated with energy for the very small bursts of time he would actually stay put. More than once, he twitched and smudged his eyeliner, his lipstick was chewed off twice, and his constant fidgeting made his eyeshadow crooked. To get his false eyelashes on, Royal held him in a headlock.

With the two of them finished and removed from my sight before I could kill Dalton, Simon sat like a gentleman statue in front of me. I blew a lock of hair from my eyes, having frizzed my hair while running my hands through it.

"Sorry," Simon said softly as I started dabbing his eyelids with primer. "He was actually doing his best, though I'm sure it didn't feel like it."

"If that's his best, I can't imagine his worst." I switched eyes and took a long breath, easing my blood pressure down.

"I hope you're never on a plane with him then. It's...rough." Simon chuckled, opening his eyes to watch me select an eyeshadow palette for him. I went back and forth between a couple of different slivers before finally dripping my brush in the right one.

When I moved to start painting his eyes, I hesitated at the look across Simon's face.

"What?"

He shook his head with a smile, something like admiration reflecting back in his eyes. "I don't know how you do it."

"Years of practice and YouTube makeup tutorials." I shrugged. "Being the little genderqueer teen gave me plenty of time to work on my cat eye and dramatic tendencies."

"Not that," Simon said around a laugh. "When my life was

flipped upside down, I was a mess. Dalton was constantly having to pull me back from nervous breakdowns, and I definitely didn't help him in a fight like you did. I overheard Royal telling Dalton about the attack and what you did with the tire iron."

"That was stupid, not brave. Close your eyes." I started dabbing on the eyeshadow carefully. "Is that how you and Dalton met?"

"Yeah." Simon smiled, keeping his eyes shut as I worked. "I was working at the Natural History Museum in New York when some cartel men broke into the lab. They were trying to take the fossil I was prepping, and I got swept up in it all. Dalton came in like..." He laughed, a sweet, genuine bubble of warmth. "Like a knight in spiky armor. He saved my life."

"How modern and romantic," I teased, smirking as he smiled.

"It sure didn't feel romantic at the time. It was terrifying and I didn't handle it well."

"I remember hearing about that. Oh, shit." I leaned back to look at him, meeting his eyes as they blinked open. "You're Dr. Andrews, aren't you? The fossil was the oviraptor egg."

"That's right."

"Wow. The articles I read about the attack didn't mention you were involved or that you got a dinosaur Romeo out of the deal."

"Thank God." Simon's smile faltered a moment. "Not about the Romeo part, obviously. I'm out now. Well, I mean I wasn't *not* out before—I just didn't know I was bi until I met Dalton. I mean thank God they didn't mention I was involved." He cleared his throat, flustered and red. "Dalton and I sort of stole it back and were on the lam for days after the attack."

"Okay." I chuckled at his sputtering and motioned for him

to shut his eyes again. "After all of that, you still work at the museum?"

"No, not anymore." Simon exhaled. "I moved out to Texas to be with Dalton."

"You gave up your job at the American Museum of Natural History?" I whistled, switching to the next shade and tapping the brush with my finger. "He must be really charming when he's not climbing the walls."

"After everything we went through, I couldn't imagine going back to my life without him."

My throat felt tight when I tried to swallow. The silver on Simon's eyelids needed blending, so I did that while I tried to find my words.

"How did you know he was worth leaving your life behind for?"

"I didn't." Simon opened his eyes when I stopped blending. "I had no idea if it was going to work. He's...wild and unpredictable. Not to mention ageless and possibly immortal."

"And a fucking dinosaur," I supplied, and he huffed an attempt at a laugh.

"Exactly. Let's not forget that."

"So." I lifted my shoulders in a shadow of a shrug. "What made you take the chance? How could you walk away from your career and life and jump into one with...a wild, immortal dinosaur with unbridled ADHD?"

Simon sighed, a lazy, content smile spreading over his face. "Dalton is...an adventure. That's all I've ever wanted in my life. Jobs come and go. Cities are just places to live. Love? A call to adventure? Isn't that the most ancient human story ever told?"

My heart stumbled over itself, tripping on a string of doubt that had been secretly tangling itself around me.

"I'm assuming you got on with another museum in Texas?" I went back to blending and adding another layer. "Working at the AMNH must have made your résumé worth its weight in gold."

"The Perot."

"Lucky. I've been clawing my way out of retail and food service for ten years. I finally got offered a job at the Royal Saskatchewan Museum doing outreach." I felt almost numb saying that, which wasn't fair. It should have made me bubble with excitement, not bittersweet longing.

"Congratulations, Blaise! That's exciting."

"Considering I have no college and am currently homeless, it's probably the best thing I'm ever going to get." I flicked my brush again to knock off the excess, the motion a little more violent than I meant it to be. "So, yeah. Pretty exciting."

"Opportunities come from strange places."

Do they, though?

I was being bitter. It wasn't Simon's fault life was hard. It wasn't his fault my career needs and my emotional needs weren't lining up. It definitely wasn't his fault that nothing was lining up for me the way I wanted them to.

And it was no one's fault but my own that I had fallen for someone who couldn't stay here while I exploded into a new career path and excelled. I had done everything on my own so far.

I could keep going alone.

There's always social media, right? I could keep up with Royal, Simon, and Dalton that way. Reach out and touch their lives digitally from thousands of miles away. Watch them on their adventures, their road trips and fossil explorations.

It would stop hurting so bad once he was gone. I'd have time to mourn and heal while doing my dream job.

Right?

That was for another time. I shoved those emotions away,

locked it in a chest labelled "yet more baggage," and tossed it into the pile with the others.

Each costume for the guys had a base theme and color palette to match their personalities. Simon was the most difficult because the poor man was a brilliant paleontologist, but had no sense of style or aesthetic. For Simon's look, he borrowed my Dolly wig, which was a huge blond monster that looked good with everything. The costume was sharp yellow and black with big shoulders to glam up the appearance.

I kept the length long to cover the fact that he had to wear flats.

Dalton's look was iridescent cellophane and neon pink striped together, with tall boots that went up to his knees. He spent the afternoon drawing raptor claws on either side of them to pull the look together. My Bubblegum wig was a large beehive that wrapped it all up perfectly.

Royal was my favorite other than my own costume.

The red sequined dress wrapped around him like silk, and the padding around his hips gave him a faux hourglass figure that worked with the mermaid-style bottom. While he couldn't rock very tall heels, the boots I found didn't make him wobble too bad if he wasn't on them too long.

The crown jewel was the ruby tiara that sat on top of my Duchess wig, which was as vibrant red as fake hair could possibly be.

"This is *perfect.*" Royal straightened the tiara on the wig and grinned, all the sparkles on his lips glittering as he did so. "I am so hot in this."

"And so modest," Simon teased, trying and failing not to adjust his breasts.

"There's no room for modesty in drag, baby." I pursed my lips in the mirror, fixing a smudge on my teeth before sliding into my own persona. God, it had been ages since I was able to be her. I missed how powerful I felt in that dress, how glam I was in full makeup, and how much I slayed with my Sera wig.

My dress was an old Poison Ivy dress recrafted for my design. Bright green and skintight, a trail of glittering leaves spiraled up from my left ankle to my right shoulder. The deadly slit up the right side let just enough leg peek out so I could show off my killer green heels. Stiletto, of course, because I was no amateur Queen. Green curls tumbled down my left shoulder, the front of the wig fixed with two big horns curving out from the cap.

Naturally, I had makeup to match. Bright, bold, and dangerous.

With all of these elements combined, Sera Bottoms was born.

I prided myself on being one of the very few dinosaur-themed Drag Queens in Canada.

The four of us, Simon Slay, Royal Majesty, Candy Raptor, and me, were ready to infiltrate the enemy base. Jush was about to get its ass slapped, and I wasn't leaving until we got what we came for.

"Alright, ladies." I snapped my fingers to get their attention. "Ground rules. When you're in drag, stay in character. Respect other queens' pronouns, or I'll break my heel off in your ass. That includes me. I'm she/her as Sera, and I will call you out for being a bitch. If something comes undone, come find me. Like previously stated, there's no time for modesty in drag. Tonight, we're all family, so don't get shy about body parts." I scanned them slowly. "Any questions?"

"Wow." Royal blinked. "You are *so* hot when you're Sera."

"Thank you." I fixed my curls. "Candy, we good?"

"Yes, ma'am!" She gave a salute. "Whatever you say, Mistress Bottoms."

"Oh, I kinda love that." I grinned. "I might need a new

outfit. Alright. If there's no questions, then let's move. The show starts in an hour, and I need a drink."

"We're not really going to, like...perform, right?" Simon followed behind us as we paraded out from the hotel room to the SUV.

"We don't have an act." I slipped into the driver's seat, since I didn't have confidence they could drive in heels. "So I fucking hope not."

"Definitely not performing," Royal confirmed. "I want to try and slip into the basement as soon as the show starts and everyone is occupied."

"What about security?" I pulled onto the road, slipping into traffic as we headed for downtown.

"They have cameras all hooked up to the cloud. I already have access to those and plan on running looped footage so they can't see anyone go down there. Dalton—er...Candy." Royal rotated in her seat to look into the backseat. "I'll run point on the floor and monitor the cameras. I want you to see if you can sneak down into the basement and find the Albertosaurus. I've run through their security and found their keycodes for the doors."

"It's something stupid like one, two, three, four, isn't it?" Candy sat up and peeled some vinyl off her left asscheek.

"Not quite. 3466. Got it?"

"Aye-aye." Candy leaned forward. "What's the plan when I find him?"

"So, we've got plans A-D." Royal ticked off fingers as she explained. "Plan A. The shifter is human and can be coaxed out the back, where Simon will be waiting with the car. That's my favorite plan. Plan B, the shifter is *not* in a coaxing mood, and we muscle him out or tranq him, then drag him outside and load him into the car."

"That's my least favorite so far," Simon grumbled. "But I have a feeling they get worse."

"Plan C," Royal continued, hesitation coating the words. "He's not in his human form, and we need to tranq an Albertosaurus, load him onto a flatbed, and get out before someone notices."

I loudly guffawed. "And plan D? Because that's a stupid-ass plan."

"Plan D is Operation Fuck It. I'm hoping we do not need this plan."

"*That's* my favorite one!" Candy bounced in her seat. I knew then and there that plan was my least favorite one.

"Only if things go tits up," Royal explained. "Otherwise, we have some solid ideas. Or at least as solid as we can for this situation."

"So what's my role?" I glanced Royal's way. "Simon's the getaway driver, you're running point, and Candy is finding the shifter. What am I doing?"

"You're a distraction if we need one." Royal smirked, her lips a fireworks display worth of sparkles. "I figured you could handle that."

"I have some tricks." I winked. "Not a problem."

A Friday night in downtown Toronto was just like any city during the weekend: crowded, loud and frantic. Parking took forever to find and was of course far away from the club. Meaning my gaggle of baby Queens had to strut a couple blocks before we could get to Jush. Because of this stroll, the plan was altered that Simon would need to start heading back to the car right after the show started, which made me thankful the poor girl wasn't in heels.

The club was bursting at the seams when we arrived, and the thrill of being around other performers and Queens made my body hum with excitement. Even though I had never been to this particular club, it felt like coming home when I saw other glam divas like myself. A small piece of me burst into warm petals of pride knowing Royal would be able to share this with me, be part of the culture I was so madly in love with.

I took her hand and squeezed. The squeeze I got back was like a tiny glitter bomb went off in my chest, filling my heart with millions of warm, beautiful sparkles.

Manning the front of the club was a big bruiser of a bouncer, checking IDs for those who looked under eighteen, but mostly flirting with the parade of color and curves. The guy was bigger than Royal, with boulders of arms and a chest King Kong would be jealous of. Long blond hair was tied back in a bun, which on anyone else would look douchey and gross.

But this guy pulled it off like a male model, and his grin was panty-melting hot.

"Evening, sheilas," he drawled as we got near, his thick Australian accent making him combustion-level hot. "Here for the show?"

"That we are, thunder from down under. You need to see my ID, or do we look old enough to ride?" I fanned my eyes at him, Royal coughing somewhere behind me.

"I think you just barely squeak by." He gave me a very appreciative onceover. His attention swiveled to a staff member asking him a question, which was answered with a smile.

His coworker gave his arm a pat. "Thanks, Kelly. I knew you'd know."

Kelly.

Why do I know that name?

The realization was a bucket of cold water down my spine.

"Welcome to Jush, ladies." Kelly swept his hand out to let us in.

"Yeah, thanks," I snapped quickly, reaching back to take Royal's hand as I rushed inside.

"Whoa, easy. I can't do this on fast mode." Royal took a teetering step to catch herself. "You okay?"

"He said his name was Kelly," I hissed softly once Royal was at my side. "He was the guy who hired those assholes who attacked you."

Royal's eyebrows were covered in makeup, so her fake ones, painted slightly higher than the real ones, rose even further up her forehead. "Oh shit."

"Yeah. Oh shit."

"At least we know we're in the right spot." She tried for a smile, but it looked uncomfortable. "Damn, he's a big one."

"Let's try and play nice."

Candy sashayed over to us with Simon around her waist. "Hey, girlies. Thor called me a dag. Is that good or bad? Who speaks Aussie?"

"Let's find somewhere to sit that puts us in the best vantage spot," Royal suggested, herding us further along inside. "Candy. That big guy is the one behind the road attacks. Stay sharp."

Candy gave Royal a wink and adjusted her costume. "Shit's sticking to my nipples."

Navigating through the mass of bodies, pointy costumes, and attachments was a struggle, but eventually, we floated from the bar to a standing table near the back. The heavy smell of latex, hairspray, perfume, and alcohol was like a balm over my nerves. Lifted voices and laughter bubbling up with the low music was the white noise of the club. Royal's fingers laced in mine, glittery lips beside my ear.

"How is it that out of so many beautiful people here tonight, you're still the most gorgeous thing I've ever seen?"

"You don't have to flirt so hard, baby. I'm already going back with you tonight."

"I'm just stating facts," Royal spoke in a low tone that traced an electric finger down my spine. "You're beautiful."

"Stay focused." I tapped her chin. "We have a dinosaur to save, right?"

Pretty painted eyes danced over my face as she nodded. "You know, this is going to be hard to believe, but this is the craziest thing I have ever done."

"You've been alive since dragonflies were as big as house-cats. How is this the craziest part of your life so far?" I stirred my drink lazily, smirking at my pretty Royal Majesty. "You can also shapeshift, so this shouldn't be that impressive to you."

"I've never stepped out of my comfort zone this far and had so much fun doing it. We've been alive this long because we're careful with risks, go with our guts, and adapt under pressure, all the pressure points of evolution since the beginning of time. This?" She displayed herself with a gesture. "This isn't something I knew how to do. We wouldn't have been able to do this without you."

"You would have figured it out," I insisted, but she shook her head, leaning in to kiss me sweetly.

"No, baby. I wouldn't have." She smiled, those fucking lips mesmerizing me. "Thank you."

"Royal..." I swallowed, dizzy from the spectacular dancing sparkles in my chest and glowing in front of me.

"Sera?" Candy leaned in beside me, biting her lip. "What do you do if you have to pee?"

"Untuck and pee." I waited, then sighed as she made a pouty puppy face. "Do you want help?"

"Yes, please."

"Okay." I finished my drink and slid it over to Royal. "Top me off, pumpkin. We're going to the ladies' room."

Candy trotted after me as I started winding my way through to the bathroom, which mercifully was large and allowed for plenty of stalls. I waved her into the last stall, holding the door like a gentleman.

"I'll be right out here if things don't want to behave."

"You're like the big sister I never had."

"Just wait until we start shaving our legs together and talking about boys," I teased, shoving her fully into the stall before shutting it. "Lord help me."

Outside the bathrooms, the muffled sounds of someone taking the stage and applause killed the music. The words were warped from the distance and walls between us and the stage, but I could gather that the MC was gearing up for the show to begin.

"Candy, how's it going in there? The show's starting." I gave the stall door a knock.

"The boys aren't behaving like before."

"Push and squeeze," I said through the door. After a couple minutes and some fabric ruffling, the toilet flushed, and Candy reappeared. "All set?"

"Yep! Do I still look delicious?" She wiggled her bottom as she washed her hands.

"Good enough to eat." I fixed my hair a bit, then motioned for her to follow. "C'mon. We both have jobs we need to be doing."

We slipped from the bathroom, cursing at the wall of static bodies shielding us from our table. I took Candy's hand and started weaseling around the other side, pushing past vinyl dresses and sequins in the hopes of making the loop. The bodies around us started to move like drag salmon up a river, and soon, Candy and I were stuck in the flow.

I realized all too late that we were being ushered behind stage.

"Oh, fuck me."

A chorus of "maybe laters" and "me first" popped off around us, and I rolled my eyes. I shimmied around to face

Candy, who was asking someone where they got their bright pink eyeshadow.

"Candy. We need to get out of here."

"Fiona is writing down the brand of the shadow she used," Candy explained as someone was scribbling across her arm. "Why do you look so freaked out?"

I opened my mouth to speak when the bodies shifted again, and my heels nearly caught the edge of some stairs.

A curvy goddess leaned down with a clipboard, her black pleather dress squeaking as she moved.

"Names?"

"We're not—"

"Candy Raptor and Cera Bottoms," Candy supplied cheerfully.

"Okay, you're on next. Tell the DJ what to play."

"Wait, we're not—fuck!" I stomped my foot as she drifted away, turning my fury to Candy. "What the fuck, Candy?"

"What?"

"They want us to fucking perform!"

She shrugged. "Okay. Didn't Royal say to run distractions?"

"*I* run distractions. *You* were supposed to scout." The last part came out through my teeth as I winked. "We don't have an act."

"Oh. Right. Crap." Her eyes widened a bit. "Whoops."

I inhaled deeply and shut my eyes. No point in turning tail and running now. We might get some stares and attention if we scrambled out in a panic. The last thing we needed was to look even the tiniest bit suspicious. If we were back here, then we were supposed to be back here, ready to take stage and dominate.

"Do you know the words to 'Shoop?'" I opened my eyes to see her snort.

"Royal is my best friend. Of course I know the words."

"Alternate verses with me. Do the slide during the chorus. Don't step on my toes." I wagged a finger at her. "I'll push you off stage, I swear to God."

"You got it, Madam Bottoms." She gave a crooked grin.

"Okay." I cracked my neck. "Tits up. Let's do this."

ROYAL

"What's taking them so long?" I tried to stretch my neck to see over the sea of bodies towards the restroom, but the tall wigs and headpieces made it impossible.

"Maybe Dalton didn't have beginner's luck twice." Simon moved some blond hair from his face. "God, I can't imagine wearing this much stuff on your face all the time. I keep wanting to scratch my eye."

"Don't smudge anything, or Blaise will tear your throat out," I said with a chuckle, but I was only half kidding. "I mean Sera. Damnit, I'm so bad at this."

"Learning curve." Simon shifted and adjusted a breast. "We're all doing our best."

"Is this where you thought you'd end up on your camping trip?"

"Oh, when it comes to going places with Dalton, I never expect anything to go according to plan." He smirked. "I'm just happy I got to see some fossils on the way here. Plus, this is fun. I love drag shows, even if I'm usually not a participant."

"Likewise." I clicked my glass against his. "For what it's worth, you look great as a platinum blond." I laughed as he rolled his eyes, the smile never falling from his face. The show started to get underway, the MC introducing a trio dancing to an old Destiny's Child song.

"Should I head back to the car?" Simon asked over the music. "Since the show started?"

"Wait until they get back. Just to be safe." I tried again to look over the crowd. "I wonder if they got stuck."

"In which way do you mean 'stuck?'" Simon winced, and I choked on my drink.

In the process of getting liquid out of my lungs and replacing it with air, I nearly swallowed my tongue when I saw who took the stage after the Destiny's Child Duo.

"Is that..." Simon blinked, his exaggerated eyes wide. "Oh dear God."

"Guess they weren't stuck," I managed around my coughing. "What the hell are they doing?"

Sera Bottoms and Candy Raptor took the stage like they belonged there, their personas on full display. The crowd was already whistling and shouting *Jurassic Park* references when the song kicked up, sending the audience into a roar.

I was honestly torn between wanting to die laughing or climb onto the stage with them. It was a tough call, to be honest. Hell, I even set my drink down like I was going to push my way through the sea of queens separating us. Ultimately, I decided not to steal their thunder and to stay with Simon.

So I watched my crush and my best friend lip-sync to "Shoop" dressed as dinosaur drag queens.

That was the moment I realized I was head over stilettos for Fredrick Blaise Fite.

The act was clearly improvised. They mixed up who was supposed to be singing, sending them into fits of play-fighting and over-the-top sass. By the middle of the song, it had turned into something like a singing battle instead of a duet. Dalton got a little too slutty with his movements. Blaise was drinking in the attention like his soul was glowing from it.

It was ridiculous and over the top.

It was perfect.

Simon bumped his shoulder against mine. "I like Blaise."

"Me too."

When it was done, Simon put his fingers in his mouth and whistled loudly. I bellowed a cheer, hoping they could hear me from the back. Dalton and Blaise bowed together, scrambling off the stage and disappearing into the back again.

"Now that we know they're not stuck and just being attention hogs, I'm heading for the car." Simon gave my arm a squeeze. "My phone's on me if plans change."

"Thanks, Simon. Be careful."

"You too." He slipped through the crowd, inching around the forest of queens around us. It was difficult to see around so many people in the dimly lit club, the sights and smells almost overpowering. Bodies, sweat, artificial flowers, and the sting of alcohol muted anything else I might have been able to take in. Flashing lights and blasting music took up my other senses.

At least the security and staff wore normal clothing. It was the only thing that stood out in the glitz and glamour of the crowd. I followed them with my eyes, my phone on the table so I could watch for any alerts from their cameras.

Anxiety tugged at my stomach with not knowing where Blaise and Dalton were. Obviously, they were safe, but I'd feel better once Blaise was at my side. Dalton could handle himself.

Hell, who was I kidding? Blaise could kick ass if he needed to. I just didn't want him to. I wanted to keep him safe.

He was herd.

Or at least I really wanted him to be.

A strong whiff of masculine cologne pierced through the haze, and I turned just as a familiar form took shape beside me. A handsome man wearing a black button-down tucked into gray slacks smiled at me, his eyes sharp and predatory. Dark curls caught the neon glow around us, the stubble on his jaw neatly trimmed around grinning teeth.

I set my jaw as I glared at him.

Ruben.

He rested his bourbon on the table and leaned in to speak over the noise of the club. A smooth voice with a rolling Spanish accent poured over the table.

"How's your back?"

CHAPTER SIXTEEN

BLAISE

That wasn't as terrible as I thought it was going to be.

In fact, we kinda fucking nailed it. Candy was kind of a hot mess at the start, but we found something of a flow once the music really got going. If we actually practiced, we may have been something close to amazing.

The highlight of the show was definitely hearing Royal's booming voice over the cheering. Through the stage light and mass of shapeless bodies in the crowd, I had no idea where he was. But hearing him made my heart do somersaults in my chest.

Departing from backstage, Candy was quickly swept up in the gaggle of people wanting to chat us up after our set. She ended up with her arm over someone's shoulder taking selfies. I slipped away, wanting to get out of the rabble and push my way back towards the table, when I noticed something very promising. Far to the back of the club, a red neon sign with scripted lettering beckoned to me.

"The Dungeon."

Two big black doors adorned with metal studs along the

edges were closed under it with a small standing sign apologizing that the dungeon was closed for the night.

I watched it for a moment, waiting to see a staff member bustling through. Casually, I strolled over to it, playing on my phone to make it seem like I wasn't paying attention. When I was close enough, I eyed it for anything that would indicate a blaring alarm. The keypad near the handle gave off a dull green glow, and I inched closer to take a look.

Glancing back towards the stage, Candy was starting to bring everyone into a round of singing a Lady GaGa song. No one was paying any attention to the pretty green Queen about to break into the Dungeon.

I held my breath as I punched in the numbers, the lock hesitating a moment before sliding free.

"Yes," I whispered, pushing the door open just enough to scan the hallway for anyone lurking nearby. Fake fire from sconces danced down the black hallway, adding to the dark taboo of what lay beyond the dungeon doors. The thumping music sealed shut behind me as I let the door slowly close. My heels echoed down the hallway after taking a step, so I slipped them off to increase my chances of staying hidden.

As if I could blend in with the gothic backdrop in my sparkling green dress and bright wig, but whatever. I was doing my best.

I had no earthly idea what the hell I was going to do if someone found me. And I kept praying to anything that would listen to a disaster like me that Royal did in fact have the cameras on a loop. I passed maybe three of them within just a couple feet of each other, each time cringing as I walked under it like the thing was bad luck. Anxiety prickled my belly; my heart was thundering in my chest worse than any stage fright I ever had.

If I got caught, would they kill me? Would they take mercy

on me if I cried? Could I drive my heel in someone's eye in a pinch? I positioned one of my shoes in my hand like a deadly weapon just in case and padded down the cold, silent stairwell at the end of the quiet hall. Just like the rest of the motif, the stairs had a gothic aesthetic of black metal, a Victorian-style railing, and textured steps. It wrapped around in a lazy spiral down into the abyss of the basement floor.

"This is stupid, this is stupid, this is *so* stupid."

Just find the shifter, call Royal, and wait. If anyone finds you, kick them in the dick and run like hell.

Easy. I could do this. Hell, I escaped worse, right? At least I wasn't running for my life in a field anymore. Nor was I being run off the road by hired assassins.

Wow, when did my life get so badass and terrible? I was a dramatic geek, not a gay James Bond. Oh, they should make one of those. Were there gay super-spy movies?

Note to self, find a gay super-spy movie. If one does not exist, email Netflix.

At the base of the long, seemingly never-ending stairwell, I found the end of the line. Another set of double doors awaited me, this time padded satin crimson with golden studs. A heavy metal bolt ran through the middle, making what would have been a sexy sight seem extremely terrifying.

No windows.

Two flickering fake torches sent orange light across the dimpled surface.

Cold seeped up from the soles of my feet, chilling my body to the bone. I didn't know how I knew, but I could feel in some very primal part of my brain that something very nasty was on the other side. Flashes of the night out in Drumheller played over in my head: giant maws of sharp teeth, larger-than-life animals growling like hissing crocodiles before snapping their jaws.

My fingers shook as I grabbed my phone, flicking it open to call Royal. Simon would be outside with the SUV. I definitely didn't want to stay down here another second, so I turned to head back up the stairs like a scared little kid escaping the creepy basement.

And wouldn't you know it.

I wasn't alone.

My phone clattered to the ground as I smacked into a broad chest, a very terrified scream ripping from me as I did. While the scream wasn't very brave or badass, I did swing my heel like a butcher knife like I had intended. Unfortunately, the big Aussie in front of me grabbed my wrist like I was a bratty child and seamlessly dodged my knee to his crotch.

"Feisty little thing, aren't you?" Kelly shoved me backwards by the wrist, bouncing me off the door. "Now, why are you down here, love? Aren't you scared of monsters?"

"I'm not into power play, asshole." His finger around my wrist was a vice, and it burned to try and wrench myself free. Each time I kicked or tried to claw at his face, he knocked my hand away or threw me off balance. "If you touch me, you'll be fucking sorry!"

"That's where you're wrong." He spun me around and pressed my face against the plush padding of the door, my arm twisted behind my back. I screamed, trying to push back and fight, but he was too damn big. The digital beeping of the keypad sent a wave of dread through my body, but it was the sound of the metal bar sliding free that filled my stomach with rocks.

Kelly's lips were close to my ear as he spoke, his low rumble like blocks of ice scraping against my spine.

"I'm not the sorry one. You are."

The door swung open, and time froze like in a horror movie.

Darkness swallowed me. Metal hinges screamed as I staggered through the doorway. I felt like I was dreaming, floating through icy waters as I fell into the mouth of the basement. The light streaming in from the hallway snapped shut like a steel trap, plunging me into a nightmare.

The dungeon didn't look anything like it had in the pictures on the internet. It was void of the kinky props or dancing poles seen in the snapshots taken by patrons months ago. Gone were the neon lights, the spinning disco ball casting stars across the floor, and the smiling faces of inebriated guests having a ball. The dull track lights high above were pointed in rays of sleepy crisscrosses, giving the dungeon more of a sad, abandoned space then anything fun and exciting.

It was empty of any signs of habitation.

Except the living embodiment of fear that slowly rose to his feet.

The lights above him rattled as the top of his skull brushed them, knocking one out of alignment as his eyes locked on me. I had never stared into the face of something so primordial and deadly, something so unmistakably predatory that my body locked up in fear. My chest tightened to the point of pain, my heart stumbling off its rhythm.

The giant Albertosaurus watched me with amber eyes, the sound of his breathing filling the steps of space between us.

For a brief, stupidly naïve, and hopeful moment, I thought maybe *Jurassic Park* got it right. Maybe if I didn't move, he wouldn't know I was there.

Then he moved. His body swayed as he took a step forward. The lights above his head clattered and spun as the dark feathers on his head lifted up slightly.

I grabbed the door handle behind me and jerked it quickly, a pathetic whimper escaping me at the resistance. Locked. Sealed.

Of course he locked me in. He was going to feed me to their captive.

My palms stung as I slammed them against the door, my throat raw as I screamed for help.

I screamed for Royal. For anyone. I begged and threatened, pulling at the door with everything I had, every ounce of strength in my body.

But it was no use. It was completely pointless.

I was going to die there. Eaten alive by the thing I had loved most my entire life.

What a fucking way to go.

Hot breath crashed against my back, and I jerked around like someone had screamed my name. Up close, the Albertosaurus's nose was dry and rough, like it was paved with thousands of little pebbles. Wide nostrils flared, the stench of sharp metallic death piercing my senses.

Blood. He smelled like blood.

I was so petrified, I couldn't even summon tears. I couldn't blink. I was laser-focused on the maw breathing in the smell of his next meal, clad in green sparkles and quivering like a rabbit in a trap.

No one was coming to save me.

I would never get to work with Laila at the museum. I would never get a chance to see more fossil sites or visit the rest of the world. I never tried Korean food.

I never told Royal I loved him.

As the Albertosaurus lifted his head, feathers raising as his mouth opened, I sucked in a sharp breath and gripped the door handle with both hands.

I wish I said something poetic or clever. I wish I declared my love for the man who stole my heart before I was eaten.

Instead, I just said, "Well fuck."

ROYAL

Ruben swirled his drink and took a sip, his eyes dancing with amusement.

"Back's fine." I took a sip of my drink. "How's the leg?"

"Sore." He tilted his head to the side. "You gave me several stitches."

"Good."

Even the guy's chuckle was annoying to me. From anyone else, I would have thought it was masculine and attractive. But with him, I just wanted to shove his glass down his throat.

I finished my drink and dropped it to the table. "So, how's this going to play out?"

"That depends. What exactly are you hoping to accomplish here?"

"I came to get the shifter you pulled from the dirt. And maybe stomp your ass for all the bullshit you've pulled at the museums and fossil sites in this country." I snarled, shaking my head. "I don't get it. Why would you slither in and desecrate our bones? Carve out chunks of our legacy? For what?"

Ruben's brows rose as he huffed a laugh. "You're thinking too small, my friend."

"I'm thinking you're a punk and a cheap shot. You destroy fossils for profit."

"How am I a cheap shot?" He eyed me with that playful smirk, like we were old friends sharing a joke.

"What do you call chomping down when someone's back is turned?"

Ruben shrugged one shoulder. "You were attacking the new kid."

"I was keeping the humans on the ground safe from a new shifter who woke up looking for a snack. You could have helped. Instead, you attacked me when my attention was on him." I leaned across the table, holding his gaze. "Didn't realize Giganotosaurus were cheap bitches."

His amuse smirk fell away, dark daggers unsheathed and aimed right at me.

"You're alive because I let you live," he growled. "If I deemed it necessary, you'd be dead and devoured."

"I've fought much bigger and a lot meaner than you, bootleg rex." I tapped the table with my knuckles. "This is how it's going to go. I'm leaving here with that shifter you plucked because I'm sure as hell not leaving him with your thieving ass. If you are this greedy about our bones, I don't trust you with anything that has a heartbeat. If you get in our way, my horn isn't going into your leg this time." I glared into his inky eyes, unflinching as he snarled. "We clear?"

Obsidian fire burned into me as he stared me down, his teeth bared ever so slightly. I didn't budge, didn't move, facing down the apex predator that dared to try and cow me into submission.

This bull didn't submit.

Not to fucking bullies and cowards.

The heat burning in his eyes ebbed, his smirk sliding back into place as he lifted his palms.

"Not a bad plan, friend. Not bad. I commend you for your effort." Ruben pulled a cell from his back pocket. "You know, when I saw you come in, I figured you had some aces up your sleeves. Well." He gestured towards me. "Skirt, maybe. So I double-checked my security system. I was very impressed with the loop and a little unnerved at how easily you cracked our defenses."

I stayed silent, wishing like hell I had Blaise in my sight. Obviously, Ruben had seen Dalton making a run for the basement, and I had no doubt he had probably sent some people after him. I only hope Dalton took care of the problem before he found the Albertosaurus in the basement.

"Making a play for the basement was a ballsy move. Though," Ruben tapped on his phone before setting it down and spinning it towards me, "I think the wrong princess ended up in the dragon's lair."

My eyes snapped to the screen, and I felt my body go cold.

Footage from a security camera inside of the basement showed clips of Blaise walking down the hallway, trotting down a long spiral staircase, and tiptoeing over to the plush red doors with a heavy bolt running through the middle. My heart seized when I saw Kelly grab him, spin him around, and shove him into the dark room.

Ruben tapped the screen, switching to a camera on the inside of the dungeon, and I saw my Blaise.

Staring at the jaws of the Albertosaurus.

Alone.

Afraid.

And about to die.

"No."

"It's too bad. She was so lovely on stage."

The cold that had frozen my body melted into a molten heat. Ruben's mouth was moving, but all noise was replaced with a high ringing of pure rage that shook my entire being. Pounding drums surfaced in my chest, my throat throbbing from the intensity of the beating.

The noise cut off like a record needle being ripped away, my vision cleared, and Ruben's voice floated into my ears.

"Let me tell *you* how this is going to go." He tried to continue, but the blood from his busted nose choked him. My skull crashed down against his face, smashing the delicate bones that made up the shape of his nose with a delightful crunch. His body flopped to the floor in pain, the crowd around us haloing out to avoid the violence.

I moved like a storm, pushing away everything in my path as I flew towards the dungeon doors to save Blaise. Nothing else mattered to me then—not my surroundings, not the shifter, not the fossils or the fact someone was chasing me. Only Blaise.

I had to get to Blaise.

A meaty hand grabbed my shoulder, ripping me from my path of destruction and throwing me against a table. Kelly rolled his shoulders back, lifting his fists up.

"C'mon, mate. You gotta do better than that." He grinned, thumbing his nose. "Big guy like you should be lots of fun."

"I don't have time for you." I pushed myself up from the table, balling my fists.

"Aw, c'mon now. I may have size over you, but you got drive. Show me what you got, you big beast."

I set my jaw, letting my fists relax. "I got something else you don't have."

"If you say Jesus, I'm going to knock you out."

"No." I lifted my chin. "I have a Dalton."

A look of dumbfounded confusion crossed Kelly's face right before a chair exploded over his back. The beefy Australian staggered forward before getting a heeled boot to his temple, knocking him motionless to the ground in a heap. Dalton snorted back in his throat and spit on Kelly's back.

"Now who's the dag?"

"Blaise is in the basement," I said as I continued towards the doors. Dalton fell in step behind me as he punched in the keycode for the door and bolted inside. The hallway seemed to stretch forever, our footsteps echoing off the hard floor and tangling with the pounding in my ears. We rushed down the stairs as fast as we could go, my heart breaking against my ribs with each second I wasn't with Blaise.

I didn't know how to prepare myself for what might be waiting for us. I didn't know how I was going to survive if we were too late.

How the hell had I let it come to this?

How could I have let him down so badly? I was supposed to protect him. Keep him safe. Keep him alive and happy.

My friend.

My herd.

My mate.

My Blaise.

"Blaise!" I rushed to the bolted door at the bottom of the stairs, my fingers shaking as I tried to punch in the code. "Blaise!"

I couldn't hear his voice, and I forced myself to believe it was the padding around the door that muted the sound.

"Blaise, I'm coming!" I cursed and tried the code again, my hand shaking too badly for me to aim my fingers correctly. The numbers buzzed red when I slipped again. "Fuck!"

Dalton pushed me aside and stabbed at the pad, grabbing my elbow and moving me back from the door as the bolt snaked free. He was already pulling his costume from his body, ready to shift as I shouldered my way through the doors like a freight train.

"Blaise!"

A couple feet away, under the crooked lights hanging from the tall ceiling, the Albertosaurus was laying on his stomach with his feet pulled up under him. His head was down like he was resting, and the echo of my shout died away into silence. My breath sawed from me as I tried to understand what I was seeing, and Dalton's hand squeezed my shoulder as I swayed on my feet.

Blaise stood by the sleeping Albertosaurus, stroking his muzzle with one hand, the other holding one finger to his lips.

I felt like passing out. Dalton steadied me as my body almost allowed it to happen.

"B?" I tried again, thinking maybe I was hallucinating.

"Shh! He's asleep." Blaise gave his nose another pat before turning towards me. "What the fuck took so long?"

Once my bones solidified again, I rushed towards him and took his shoulders, looking him over for injuries. No blood. No cuts. No bite-sized chunks taken out of him.

Hell, his makeup was still perfect.

"Fuck," I exhaled, pulling him into my arms and holding him tight. "I thought I lost you. Jesus jumping Christ, B. Why are you down here?"

"I wanted to find Al. Candy had everyone's attention, so I went for it." Blaise wrapped his arms around my neck and squeezed. "I'm okay, Royal."

I reluctantly let him go, eyeing the sleeping giant to the right of me. "How did you do this?"

"Maybe he's like a tyrannosaur whisperer," Dalton offered. "Did you make a 'tss' noise and poke him in the neck?"

Blaise shook his head, his hand stroking Al's nose. "He's just scared."

"Scared?" My eyebrows tried to reach my wig. "How do you know?"

"Well, I thought he was going to eat me. So when he stuck his nose in my face, I slapped it and started yelling at him, and he just...laid down. Then I felt bad and started petting him. Then he fell asleep."

"I have...no words," I finally admitted after staring at the massive beast curled up on the floor. "I honestly don't know what to say."

Dalton walked around Al, studying the drowsy dinosaur before giving an amused giggle.

"That's not why." He slipped his wig off and shucked the rest of his costume. "I'll show you."

"What in hell are you doing?" Blaise wrinkled his nose, looking very unimpressed as Dalton tipped his tape away and shook himself loose.

"Just watch."

"No." Blaise snorted, turning his head. "Seen it. Don't care."

I barked a laugh, and Dalton flipped me off.

"Not my peen, you pervert. Watch what I'm *about* to do." Dalton paused, then lifted a finger. "And I'll have you know, my peen is very impressive, and my boyfriend likes it. So." He gave a raspberry with his tongue before beginning to shift. Blaise glanced towards him for just a moment when his bones began popping and sliding but covered his eyes in horror as his skin stretched and started sprouting feathers.

Dalton's human form warped and twisted into something ancient yet familiar, his black feathered body huge, strong and mighty, with a long tail fanned with white-tipped feathers. Instead of a beak like his bird cousins, his snout was long with rows of dagger teeth. An iconic, sickle claw was on each foot, and his sharp, icy blue eyes flexed as he looked at us.

"Holy shit," Blaise breathed. "I forgot you're a raptor."

Dalton squawked, shaking himself out as Al cracked his eyes open. Al's big head lifted as he looked at Dalton, nostrils flaring as he smelled the newcomer.

Dalton pranced a bit, fluffing out his feathers a bit before turning his face towards the fellow theropod. He lifted a proud line of feathers from his head, a bright pink ridge like a mohawk that once served as his display of ferocity and vitality.

Al watched him carefully, the feathers around his neck and on his skull ruffling out in response.

Then I saw what Dalton was referring to.

Al's dark, pebbling skin blended well with the deep, iridescent black feathers that rested like a lion's mane around his head. But when they flared out, they shone a brilliant, vibrant color.

Green.

Bright fucking green.

"Oh." I sighed.

"What?" Blaise looked at me, his attention pingponging between the dinosaurs and me.

"He thinks you're pretty. Or a baby. I don't speak theropod."

"...Beg pardon?" Blaise leaned towards me in surprise, but I didn't have time to explain. The dungeon doors swung open with a crash, and a very pissed-off, bloody Ruben stormed in. Blood smears down his mouth and chin made his glare more intense, like he had just ripped someone apart with his teeth rather than taken a beating.

"You want to play it this way?" He sneered, tearing off his shirt and sending buttons skittering across the floor. "Fine. This time, I'm not letting you live."

"B." I guided him behind me with my hand, my eyes locked on the inbound threat. "Get to a corner and stay there. Dalton."

Dalton swung his head to me, his feathers raised and teeth bared.

"Operation Fuck It."

He squawked loudly, and I started to shift.

CHAPTER SEVENTEEN

BLAISE

This was the third or maybe fourth time I had seen Royal shift, and I still wasn't used to it.

The way the skin stretched over the writhing, bone-crunching chaos made my stomach churn as it was, but having it in stereo made it so much worse. Ruben was noisier when he transformed, letting out a horrible scream of rage that warped into a hissing nightmare as he grew. My feet felt glued to the ground as I stared up at the heroes of my childhood squaring off against each other. Horns were lowered, feathers ruffled, and so many teeth were bared.

When Ruben launched himself at Royal, my feet finally came free.

I turned and ran like hell to avoid being swept up in the battle. The sound of bodies colliding mixed with animal groans of pain made my stomach line with ice. The basement was big, but it wasn't nearly gigantic enough for four dinosaurs to have a full-on brawl.

Light fixtures were torn down as Ruben's big head crashed into them, raining sparks down around them as Royal shoved him backwards with his head. The Giganotosaurus staggered back, snapping his jaws at Royal. Dalton scurried up Ruben's already pounded leg, ripping into him with his claws and teeth, and barely escaped before Ruben could crunch his mouth around him.

I could feel stress lines forming on my face from watching the fight, trying to shrink down in a corner. Al rose to his feet when the fighting started, and I sucked in my breath in horror. Two massive theropods against my boys didn't seem like a fair fight, even if Royal and Dalton were vicious fighters.

"Hey!" I screamed, jumping up and down, my voice barely lifting above the carnage. Al snapped his jaws at Dalton as he got too close, his sights focusing on Royal as he fought for his life.

Was this what Dr. Grant felt like? Was I a sexy drag Dr. Grant?

I panicked. The helplessness of the situation sent my body into action before I thought better of it. I grabbed one of my heels and threw it as hard as I could into Al's ankle, screaming at him to look at me.

When his sharp, amber eyes landed on me, I started waving my arms and backing away from the fight. Royal had said he felt connected to me somehow, and I certainly hoped I was still something of value to the big, annoyed-looking Albertosaurus glaring at me.

Would he eat me? Would he try and take care of me?

Oh God. I hoped he didn't think I was flirting. I wouldn't survive that date.

Al's eyes flexed, and he moved his nose as he studied me, backing away.

"That's it. Come along. Good dinosaur." I beckoned him with my hands. "Please don't fucking eat me, okay? I'm nice, remember? I gave you nose pats."

Royal's big body crashed into the wall as Ruben shoved him

backwards with his tail, and I let out a scream of alarm. Al's focus on me shifted, and his feet went into motion. He came at me fast, too fast, and I scrambled backwards before falling on my ass. I crab-walked backwards until my back slammed up against the wall, Al's rapid footsteps closing in on me in just two or three steps. I ducked my head, covering myself with my arms, and waited for teeth to descend on me.

The sound of meat hitting the floor made me scream again, and I peeked out from behind my arms to see Al had put himself in front of me and the fight.

He was shielding me.

"Oh thank fuck." I put my hand on my chest, allowing myself a moment of calm, and checked to make sure I didn't piss myself.

I hadn't, for the record. But it had been close.

Royal's bellowing scream turned my blood to ice, and I rushed around Al to see what was happening. Al used his big nose to nudge me closer to him like a wandering chick, and I nearly crashed to the ground again.

Royal's side was bleeding, teeth marks punctured into him like before. Blood was dripping from his hide to the floor, mixing with the slippery smears from Ruben's busted-up leg. Dalton's feathers looked wet, and he fluffed them out as he hissed.

The smell of blood hung in the basement air like a sack of wet pennies. Their hot breath mixed with the stench and made my stomach curl. Ruben's back leg buckled slightly as he took a step, but he corrected his posture as he slowly circled Royal. A mouth of steak knives opened in threat, spit hanging down from his chin. Royal pushed to his feet, nose flaring as he gulped down air.

Dalton made a high chattering noise, his tail feathers fanning while his pink ridge stood up tall. Royal's shoulders squared, and he flattened his frill down against his neck to protect himself from Ruben's jaws.

My mind raced with frantic flashes of what could be. Images of Royal's frill folding under Ruben's jaws kept repeating in my head. The Giganotosaurus was too big. He was going to rip Royal apart in such a small space, and there was nothing I could do.

I wanted to scream. To fight. If I could have managed a way up Ruben's body, I would have stabbed him in the eye with my heel.

But I couldn't. I was fucking helpless.

Everything happened so fast after that. In that moment of soul-crushing defeat, the fight swung the other direction.

Dalton sprinted like black lightning, springing up into the air onto Royal's frill. Royal flung Dalton through the air like a lacrosse ball, sending the hissing bundle of feathers directly into Ruben's face. Claws, teeth, and chaos slashed at Ruben's face like a feathery nightmare, sending the beast spiraling away in pain. Blinded and unable to reach tiny arms up to knock the raptor from his face, Ruben swung his head around trying to throw him off.

Giving Royal the opening he needed.

The bull Regaliceratops huffed out and sent his tank-like body right into Ruben's ribs, sending him careening over like a ragdoll. The mighty theropod rolled once, smacking against the basement wall before falling onto the floor in a heap.

Dalton trotted away from him, rushing to Royal's side as they prepared themselves for another round, bloody and winded from the fight.

Ruben let out a long, pained groan, his bad leg unable to lift him off the ground. He lifted his head and growled deep in his throat, before letting it fall back to the ground.

There was a long pause, like the room as a whole held its

breath for what would happen next. My chest burned as I finally inhaled at seeing Ruben shrink down to his beaten human form. Dalton and Royal soon followed, the shift apparently painful when you have injuries. Royal swore and held his side, and Dalton hissed as he touched a bloody bite mark near his neck.

"I was going to get a tattoo here next week, you asshole," Dalton spat. "I'm running low on real estate."

Ruben coughed and held his ribs, blood coating his teeth.

Royal glared down at him, still catching his breath. "We're done. You don't follow us. You don't fuck with us." He pointed towards Al and me. "They're with us now. If you come after either one, I'll kill you."

Ruben spit some blood to the side and nodded. "I hear you, herbivore. You've made your point."

"That's *Mister* Herbivore to you, punk," Dalton snarled. Ruben gave him an unamused stare.

"Royal!" I rushed to his side, fretting over the gashes in his skin. "Jesus. Those look deep."

"I'm okay. They just look bad, but my insides are fine. Whoa—B, no." His big arms caught me before I could kick the shit out of Ruben.

"Get up so I can kick you in the dick!"

"Easy. B. Ow, baby, please." Royal hissed, and I stopped wiggling, remembering his wounds.

"Shit. Sorry! I'm sorry." I pointed at Ruben. "Fuck you." Then I turned back to Royal. "I'm so glad you're okay. We need to get the hell out of here."

"Yeah. But what about Big Al?" Dalton hiked a thumb behind his shoulder. "He's still stuck on big mode."

Royal winced and took my hand, walking with me back towards the huge Albertosaurus watching us.

"Montana told me that new shifters are hypersensitive to

body language. They can tell when we come at them with aggression or submission." He squeezed my fingers. "I think that's why he wanted to protect you. He could tell you were scared."

"*Scared* is a catastrophic understatement," I mumbled.

Royal smirked, pain still painting over his features. "He needs to know not to be afraid. Maybe he'll listen to you."

"I also don't speak theropod, Royal."

"I think you speak Al." He paused in front of the big dinosaur watching us. "It's kinda the only shot we have."

No pressure.

I exhaled, feeling the weight of the situation press down on my shoulders.

"Make a Hulk reference!" Dalton called from across the basement, and Royal hushed him.

Al watched me, his golden-hued eyes tracking my movement over his snout. His nose was dry, warm and rough, like running your fingers over sunbaked, leathery concrete.

"I know you don't understand me," I admitted to him softly. "And I've been told that we look like scary squids when you first wake up. If I had the choice between being a bigass apex dinosaur or a small, genderqueer mess with deep abandonment issues, I'd likely stick with the first option. But it's not all that bad. There's art, culture, love, and so much good food. You have to trust me, which is asking a lot." His nose felt like stone against my forehead. "And I promise I'll name you something better than Al. But you have to change."

"That's beautiful, B," Royal rumbled from behind me. "Well said."

I smiled, giving Al's nose a pat. A long blast of hot breath blew against my dress, and I squeaked at the sensation. The nose I was leaning on shifted backwards, and I staggered forward at the loss. Royal steadied me with his arm around my waist, and we watched as Al shrank down from a giant tyrannosaur to a worried-looking man.

Al's shaggy brown hair stuck up like he slept badly, his white skin flushed with fresh goosebumps as he shivered from the cold. His pretty amber eyes stayed the same color, looking at me for guidance.

"Hey." I held out my free hand for him. He hesitated, his gaze bouncing from me to Royal, who was smiling gently.

"It's okay," Royal agreed. "Let's go home."

Al took a couple of steps, his huge body thick with muscles tensed from the cold as he placed his hand in mine. I gave it a squeeze, and he grunted.

Dalton hit the button for the wide warehouse doors resting in the very back of the room, the metal gears whirring to life to lift them. The back wall of the dungeon jerked and rose, exposing us to the street outside behind the club, where Simon waited for us in an idling car. The driver door swung open when he saw the state of Dalton, and Simon rushed over to check on his bloody boyfriend.

"Oh my God, Dalton. Is that a bite? Royal, Jesus, you look like someone attacked you with a cheese grater. And—ah. Oh. Hello." Simon cleared his throat, looking anywhere but towards Al's crotch.

Al stared at him, bewildered.

"Simon, this is Al. We're changing his name immediately." I gestured between Al and Simon. "That's Simon."

Al didn't reply. He looked very unsure of everything.

We were ushered away from the garage and to the waiting vehicle, and Simon dug out the first-aid kit that was buried under their camping gear and a couple suitcases. Al was given a blanket to wrap up in, and I volunteered to drive us back to the hotel.

We had to be quite the sight rolling up to the hotel, three-fifths of us naked, two bloody, two still in full drag, and one only grunting. Wild night on the town in Toronto, that's for sure.

All of us piled in one room, the first-aid kit between the bloody shifters, who whined when Simon and I cleaned them up. Dalton pouted about his tattoo needing to be moved, holding some ice to his hip where he landed badly in the fight.

Poor Royal was sore and tired, his skin tender and ripped up by Ruben's teeth. The slices weren't as deep as they could have been due to his thick ceratopsian hide, but they still looked painful.

"Stop wiggling." I dabbed at the wounds after flushing them out. "I know it burns, but you're squirming too much for me to patch you up."

"I'm going to be chewed-up-looking after this," Royal groaned into his pillow, laying on his good side for me to work. "Do you like scars? Do I look manly and badass or like a Rottweiler's chew toy?"

"Very manly." I winced as he hissed through teeth, the bandage I was taping down pulling on tender skin. "Sorry. Still manly."

"So." Dalton leaned his head towards Al, who was staring blankly at the flickering television. "How are we going to handle the big guy over there?"

"Is he going to shift again?" Simon sounded worried as he eyed the hunched man trying to understand the late-90's sitcom with the canned laugh track.

"I don't think so." Royal shook his head, carefully sitting up. "He can stay with us tonight since he's pretty attached to Blaise. The trip home will be...exciting."

"We're not flying, right?" Dalton paled. "Because if he's like me on planes, that's a bad idea."

"Hell no," Royal agreed. "No planes. You're bad enough.

I'm not dealing with two theropods freaking out in a flying tin can. We'll drive."

"That's a long trip," Simon said with a heavy sigh. "A couple of days at least."

"Nah, it'll be fun. We haven't seen the petting zoo I wanted to see last time." Dalton grinned, pulling Simon into his lap to kiss his cheek. "Don't worry about it. It's like an extension of our vacation."

"Family road trip," Royal sang, sounding exhausted down to his bones, but smiling all the same.

"Yeah, sounds like a blast." Simon tried to go for a dry delivery, but his laugh made it land lighthearted. "Let's get back to our room so they can rest."

Dalton hauled himself to his feet, adjusting the towel around his waist so he could make the walk to their room without flashing anyone. He turned and flashed a toothy grin at us. "We did good tonight, gentle-folx. Royal, my man, you kicked ass. B, my sassy queen, you shook ass. We need to party more."

With a salute, the pink-mohawked raptor and his tired paleontologist slipped out of our room.

I spent way too long in the shower after they left. My makeup needed to be scrubbed off my face, my body was tight with tension from the *multiple* times I thought my life was ending that night, and I needed to let the decently hot hotel shower soak my aching muscles. With the chaos done, the day saved, and the bad guys defeated, all that was left now was the part I didn't want to face.

The goodbye.

Maybe that's the real reason I hid away in the bathroom as long as I did. The thought of facing Royal now, having to tear away from the connection I had made with him, felt like it would kill me. I loved him. I loved his family. And Al was kind of like my adopted, giant foster kid now.

Having to watch them drive away without me the next morning was going to rip me into tiny, sad ribbons.

I didn't know how I was going to see the other side of it. But maybe once the job started with Laila, I would have something to distract myself from the horrible loss I was about to face down.

By the time I left the bathroom, Royal was passed out on his stomach across the bed. Al was curled up on the floor by the TV with his blanket half on his torso. A wash of relief fell over me knowing I had one more night with them. Nothing had changed yet. I could pretend this was my normal night.

Okay, I could have done with less blood and mayhem, but they were cute and calm when they're sound asleep.

I tucked a pillow under the sleeping Albertosaurus's head and added a blanket over him. I wasn't sure how we were going to convince him to put on clothing, but that was tomorrow Blaise's problem.

With my foster dinosaur covered, I slowly climbed into bed next to the love of my life. Royal's long lashes fanned over his cheeks in his slumber, the smell of antibacterial spray and bandages mixing with the scent of his skin. I slipped my hand under his palm and laced our fingers together.

Tonight, he was mine.

Tomorrow...

I didn't want tomorrow.

CHAPTER EIGHTEEN

ROYAL

The only thing that hurt worse than my shredded side and sore skull was the unspoken conversation between Blaise and me.

I had woken up feeling like I had been dragged behind a truck over a field of razors and salt, but had Blaise cuddled up next to me. I stayed in bed much longer than I should have, ignoring my screaming bladder and roaring stomach, just so I could watch him sleep a little longer. There was no telling how the rest of the morning was going to go, and I wasn't in a rush to meet the less-than-favorable scenarios.

When he did wake up, his eyes fluttered open and blinked sleepily at me. A small, sweet smile tugged at the corner of his mouth as I stroked his soft hair between my fingers. I didn't comment when he couldn't stop a tear from falling from one eye, only kissed the tip of his nose.

I hope he knew I felt the same.

We were finally forced out of bed when Al pissed in the corner of the room. I jumped up to steer him towards the bathroom. Blaise threw a towel over the mess, yelling in horror as he did.

Ah, new shifters. It's like having a man-sized puppy. The potty training would be tough, but the teething part, I had been told, was the real treat. Theropods liked to chew things, mark territory, and were known to be food-aggressive.

So. A big puppy. That could turn into a dinosaur on a whim.

While Blaise got Al to put clothing on and parked him in front of the TV, I grabbed us breakfast and changed out my dressings. Al growled once at Blaise when he gave him food and immediately folded when Blaise wagged a finger at him and told him to behave.

It was hilarious and kinda hot.

Blaise flicked over his phone while we ate, glancing up at me after he finished his eggs. "What do you think about Henry?"

I swallowed my coffee. "What?"

"Instead of Al, he can be called Henry."

"Why Henry?"

Blaise slid his phone over to me, which was open to the Wikipedia page on Albertosaurus. "Because if we go with the normal naming convention your team uses, his name would be Horseshoe."

"Unique names build character," I teased and smirked when he gave me a look from hell.

"Mkay. We're going to call him Henry, after the paleontologist who named Albertosaurus." A flash of melancholy fell over his face for a moment, dulling the glow in his eyes. "Let him know I picked the name after he gets a grasp on the language."

"B." I set my plastic fork aside just as he got up, busying himself with collecting the remnants of our breakfast.

"I know." Blaise buzzed around the room, distracting himself. "I don't want to do this yet."

That sent a knife into my heart, the sting more severe than the chew marks on my side. I forced myself up, aiming to catch the floating butterfly that was avoiding my gaze, when Dalton's rhythmic knocking came at the door. With a sigh, I pulled it up and lifted my chin.

"Hey, man."

"Simon's got the car all packed with our crap. I called Daddy Montana and let him know we got baby brother Al and we're hitting the road within the hour." He leaned on the door-frame. "You need help getting everyone's stuff into the car?"

"Al's name is Henry now. B picked it for him."

"Henry. Cute. Okay, then. You want me to wrangle Henry while y'all pack?" Dalton's blue eyes held mine, and his voice dropped into a whisper. "Wasn't sure how many bags are going into the car."

I swallowed down the knot in my throat and took a breath. "Can you take Henry and give us a little bit?"

"Sure." Dalton clapped me on the shoulder and moved inside. "Henry. Oh, hey, you got pants on. Welcome to Human 101. Wait until we show you video games and porn. You're gonna love it."

Henry grunted, looking for Blaise for guidance as Dalton took his hand. He only followed Dalton's lead when Blaise nudged him to comply, and Dalton shut the door behind them.

The hotel grew painfully quiet then. Blaise wrapped my hoodie around his small frame and hugged his chest, his eyes glued to the floor.

"I knew you were going to leave," he whispered, his voice watery as soon as he spoke. "You were very clear about that. I knew what I was getting into." His throat clicked as he swallowed, shoulders pulled up to shield himself. "It still hurts."

Seeing him shrink into himself, hearing the pain lacing his words, it tore at my heart like a thousand little papercuts at once. My head was reciting the same mantra of logic over and over, all the while my heart bled.

His life was here. His *career* was here.

I had no right to be so goddamn selfish.

Despite knowing, absolutely knowing, what the right thing to do was, I still found myself driven by the bleeding muscle beating in my chest.

"Blaise." I sat on the edge of the bed and pulled him over by his wrists gently, gazing up at him to try and meet his gaze. His eyes were shut, lashes wet, jaw jumping as he tried to contain the same emotions ripping me to pieces. My thumbs traced the small bones of his hands, and I could remember how his fingers felt laced through mine.

I steadied myself with a long breath before I continued.

"Would I be the biggest jerk on the planet if I asked you to come with me?"

His exhale was shaky, tears falling down his flushed cheeks. "Would I be making the biggest mistake of my life if I went? I've dreamed about this job for so long, Royal. I never thought I'd get it."

"I know. And I can't say whether or not you would get this chance again. I can't promise that. But, B. Hey." I reached up and wiped a tear away, finally catching his eyes with mine. Wet hazel eyes pleaded with me, hopeful and terrified. "If you come with me, with us, you wouldn't be doing this alone. You'd be with me, with my family. We'd stand with you every step, help you find something you want to do." I laughed. "You don't need me to save you. You've proven that. But if you let me stand with you, I will. You can be my herd. I...I love you, Blaise."

"You've known me five minutes," he whispered, sounding unsteady.

"That's all it took."

When he threw his arms around my neck and kissed me, it was the most brilliant feeling of warmth I had ever felt.

Followed by a sharp stabbing pain from my side being

jostled. The moment was mildly wilted by me hissing and him jerking back in alarm.

"Oh, shit. Shit. I'm sorry, I'm so sorry. Are you okay?"

"I'm fine," I managed between a pained laugh mixed with a groan. "Is that a yes or are you trying to kill me?"

His slim fingers took my face in his hands and brought our lips together. Sweet, wonderful kisses peppered my mouth, his lips tinted with the salt from his tears.

"Don't break my heart, Royal," Blaise whispered against the kiss. "I won't make it if you do."

"Never," I promised, pressing my brow against his.

Blaise huffed out a laugh against my lips, sniffing back tears and dashing them away with his fingers. "Okay. I'll come with you." He swallowed and ran his thumbs over my jaw. "Isn't Texas really hot and mostly cowboys, though?"

"You already said yes." I pulled him into my lap. "No takies-backies."

"Dammit." He looped his arms around my neck, a smile still curling his lips.

"There is still one hurdle we have left." I winced, looking up at him. "Montana."

"Oh." Blaise lifted his eyebrows. "Is he going to be okay with me being there?"

"Yeah." I attempted to lie, but Blaise saw right through it. "Probably."

"Royal."

"Dalton brought Simon home. He'll come around." I gave his hip a pat. "C'mon. We have a lot of cases to pack up."

BLAISE

I wasn't fond of being someone's secret.

I'd lived that life. It usually ended in heartache and someone slashing my tires. To be fair, the secret was a secret to me too. I wasn't a homewrecker on purpose, only on accident and by guys with bad tattoos and clean sideburns. It's a weird statistic.

Having Dalton and Simon on my side helped my unease. They seemed genuinely happy that my bags were being packed in the back of the car, and when Dalton kept talking about the tacos back home in Texas, I started feeling better. Each time a spike of nerves would ripple through my stomach, Royal squeezed my hand and told me that he loved me.

It helped. He helped.

Laila was disappointed when I told her I wasn't coming, but my reasoning seemed to sit better with her than I would have thought.

"If I was going to ride into the sunset with someone, he'd look like Royal too," she had texted back. "Tell him to take care of you, B. And if you need a recommendation for work, reach out." Then she signed it with hearts.

Simon turned around in the passenger seat to look at me. I was sandwiched between my boyfriend (it still felt amazing to call him that) and my foster theropod. Henry watched outside zooming by as closely as he had the TV, his honey-colored eyes skipping over the horizon.

"How did she take it?" Simon nodded towards my phone. "Was she disappointed?"

"Yeah, but she understood." I ran my thumb over Royal's knuckles, and he kissed my temple. "I'm happy to be coming to Texas, but I can't help but feel like I just walked away from something lifechanging."

"I felt that way when I left New York," Simon agreed. "It's terrifying. And my friends and family were kinda pissed for like a month. But ultimately, it was exactly what I needed." He smiled as Dalton squeezed his knee. "And Blaise, I don't know if this would interest you, but I work at the Perot. I can get you a meeting with our head of marketing. Maybe they can find a spot for you."

"Really?" I sat up in my seat, the sour dread in my stomach warming into something hopeful.

"It's not a guarantee, but I'll help where I can. I'll help you get your foot in the door at least." Dimples dented in his cheeks when he smiled. "It'll be nice to have another fossil nerd around."

"Thanks, Simon. That really helps." I relaxed back against Royal, exhaling a calming breath as his arm looped over my shoulders. Maybe it wouldn't be so bad. Maybe I had another shot at something great in Texas.

What the hell was I saying?

I had the best shot at everything I ever wanted.

I had good friends. A makeshift family made up of paleontologists and dinosaurs. A possible career track or at least a start to something wonderful.

And I had a handsome, loving, hot-as-hell boyfriend who loved me.

What else could I ever want?

Like any good family road trip, we had a healthy mixture of laughing, singing, bickering, one instance of Henry scaring some strangers at a gas station, a flat tire, getting lost, and Royal hacking into someone's phone at a gas station and changing their loud, thumping music to polka for fun.

All in all, it was an enjoyable trip across North America. I could have done without Dalton's driving for a couple stretches, but otherwise, it was great.

Texas was what I expected it to be.

Flat. Hot. Lots of cows. Killer bar-be-que and long stretches of nothing that exploded into cities. Dallas was a blast of glass and chrome that tangled into car-clogged veins running through the center. There was so many unique places to eat, bursts of color, music, and culture striped through various sections of the city, and so much damn traffic. But it seemed fun and like a city I'd learn to love.

The RELIC estate was a couple miles north of Dallas proper on a huge plot of land in the middle of nowhere. A gate kept outsiders from coming near the property without permission, cameras posted along the fencing to make sure their secrets were safe. Behind the giant house was a dense forest beyond a long stretch of land, where they "frolicked and played" in the mornings, according to Dalton.

The house itself was huge. Three stories and gorgeous, with wide windows to let the sun stream inside. All of our bones popped and creaked as we climbed out of the car, the late afternoon sun hanging lazily above us as we unpacked. Henry stood outside the car smelling the air, annoyed he couldn't make sense of anything.

A thick Middle Eastern man emerged from the house as we pulled up, a scowl plastered across his face when he saw Henry and me. He gestured harshly at us and turned his black eyes to Dalton and Royal.

"Who the fuck are they?" His Arabic accent lifted his words, which was a beautiful contrast to how pissed he looked.

"Baha, this is the new shifter, Henry. Albertosaurus." Royal nodded to Henry, who watched him warily. Then Royal took my hand. "And this is my boyfriend, Blaise."

"Hi." I gave a little wave.

Baha stared at me a long time, then mumbled in Arabic, running a hand down his face.

"Be nice, Grumpysaurus," Dalton scolded from the trunk. "He's cool."

"You're a Spinosaurus, right?" I tried, thinking maybe it would help the situation like a dumbass. It didn't help. Baha's head snapped up, and he went off in Arabic, his hands going wild.

"Hey!" Dalton threw an empty bottle at him. "Language!"

"This is going well," I muttered, leaning into Royal.

"Baha." Royal met his gaze, his voice low. "Stop being a prick. I just said he was my boyfriend, not a stranger. Be respectful, brother. We welcomed Jackson and Simon in."

Baha inhaled through his nose and eyed me again. "You know about us?"

"Yeah." I summoned my courage and held his coal-black eyes. "I do. I left everything behind to be here with him and to meet his family. I get that you don't like strangers, but I'm not going anywhere. I love your brother and don't have to prove shit to you."

Simon gasped, covering his mouth. Dalton made the low "ooo" sound like when kids got in trouble. Royal laughed. Henry growled.

Baha squinted his eyes at me, then looked at Royal. "I like this one."

My confidence swelled, but quickly deflated when someone else walked out of the house.

Even without knowing who he was, I knew he was Montana. I knew he was someone powerful, ancient, and strong. Deep blue eyes studied us like how a cat studied mice, his body language the relaxed stroll of a predator at the top of the chain.

If that wasn't enough, Henry went from being a growling brat to a stock-still, silent statue.

He knew.

And he wasn't giving the T.rex any reason to be mad at him.

I had flashbacks of how he submitted to Ruben, lowering

himself and going docile. I couldn't tell if he was afraid, or if it was something else entirely.

Montana's eyes swept from Henry to me, then lifted up to Royal.

"Hey, boss." Royal swung out clasped hands. "This is Blaise."

I swallowed.

"He just told Baha off. You missed it," Dalton added unhelpfully.

Having a staring contest with a T.rex was about as terrifying as it sounds, even when he's not in his big form. Montana had the unwavering glare of a timeless predator who never knew fear. I had to lift my chin to meet his eyes when he walked over to us, his voice cool, calm, and serious.

"I know about the livestream."

It took me entirely too long to cough out, "Sorry."

"How do I know I can trust you?" His deep blue eyes narrowed. "How do I know that you won't film us here? Spread more of our secrets out onto the web for views?"

Royal's hand squeezed mine, sending a bolt of courage through me that squared my shoulders.

"Because I love Royal, and I wouldn't do anything to hurt him. Simon and Dalton are like the sweet, nerdy, and insane brothers I never had, and Henry is like my adopted, terrifying son, and I'm immediately invested in him. Plus." I gestured towards him. "You're a fucking T.rex. If I screw up, you'll probably eat me."

Montana pierced through me with his unnerving stare, standing so still I wasn't sure if he was breathing. When he finally did speak, it almost made me jump.

"There is no probably. I will. Remember that." He lifted his chin towards the bodies around us. "This is my family, Blaise. My brothers. I will rip you into tender pieces if you cause them pain. But," Montana paused, nodding to Royal, "if Royal wants you here, I won't turn you away."

"Thanks, HC." Royal spoke softly, a smile on his lips.

"HC?" I bounced my eyes between them. "What's HC?"

"Hell Creek. It's his code name."

"So badass," I whispered.

Montana's gaze shifted from stony to exhausted as he pinched the bridge of his nose. "Are all of you going to be coming back from missions with boyfriends?"

"You think someone's gonna follow Yu back here? I mean Yu the guy named 'Yu,' not you-you. I think a guy would be lucky to have you, boss. And I mean you, not the guy named Yu —" Dalton spiraled, and Baha snapped his fingers.

"Fucking stop."

"What do you expect?" I smiled some. "You have really handsome brothers."

"He's got a point," Royal agreed. "We're pretty cute."

"Get in the house," Montana grumbled. He turned his attention to Henry. He hadn't moved from his spot. Henry's amber eyes watched him as Montana carefully approached, the confident stride easy and calm. Henry didn't shy away, but he did inch back a fraction when Montana lifted his hand and placed it against Henry's chest.

There was a long pause, the two tyrannosaurs staring at each other. An unspoken, apex language I didn't know passed between them. Montana moved close and put his other hand behind Henry's head, connecting their foreheads. Henry's eyes shut, and he exhaled, his shoulders dropping.

"What's happening?" I whispered to Royal, watching the two together.

"He's letting him know he's safe," he answered softly. "Have you ever seen parrots putting their heads together and cuddling? It's a theropod thing."

"That is painfully adorable."

"Yeah." Royal squeezed my hand, kissing the top of my hair. "Let's go inside so I can show you our place. Maybe after a shower, some pain meds, and dinner, we can get a little more *comfortable.*"

I grinned up at my hunky, dinosaur boyfriend. "Good idea."

EPILOGUE
ROYAL

"This was a great idea." Simon was smiling wide as we watched Sera with the kids. "Who knew that Dino Drag Story Time would be such a success?"

"She did." I smirked. "She rarely has bad ideas."

Sera sat in a chair with her legs crossed, a new sparkling green dress draped over her that stopped just above her sharp heels. The new lime wig was done up in a cute bob, with glittery white horns and a golden frill that perched on the back. It almost looked like a crown sitting back far on her head, and it caught the light brilliantly.

The kids shouted their favorite dinosaurs and called out lines from the book as she read it to them, showing them the pictures as she did. It was a cute, illustrated kid's book about the Cretaceous, and the young, dinosaur-obsessed crowd was eating it up. Sera had the perfect mixture of sass and humor to keep the kids engaged, and her bright outfit made the kids instantly love her.

The Perot held Dino Drag Story Time once a month in the downstairs lobby, next to the Malawisaurus skeleton. This was one of the new ideas brought to the table once Blaise had been hired on as their community outreach assistant, and it had taken off like wildfire. There also had been talk of a science-themed fair that Laila helped Blaise plan out over Zoom calls and late-night emails.

I had been tasked with hauling around Sera's bags for these events and been volun-told that I'd be helping build things for the fair once it got off the ground. It was a job I was very happy to have.

Once the reading was done, I hung back to let Sera meet her adoring fans before she finally made her way to me. She happily drank some water and moved some hair from her cheek.

"The kids today were wild," she said after taking a drink. "I thought that little girl was going to vibrate through the floor, she was so excited."

"She loves you. Almost as much as she loves pachyrhinosaurus, apparently."

"Who doesn't?" She smirked. "Hey, I was given next weekend off. Did you still want to head down to Glen Rose?"

"Hell yeah. You'll love it." I slipped her hand into mine, shouldering her bag. "Also, Montana wants me to travel out to Louisiana next month on a lead. There's been talk about some mosasaur teeth being sold off as black magic charms or something. Sounds spooky. Want to come?"

"Um, *yes*." She scoffed. "That sounds amazing. Give me just a bit to undress, and let's grab some lunch." She kissed my cheek, taking the heavy bag from me before disappearing into the employee area. Normally, when Sera got done with a show, it took her an ungodly amount of time to undress and strip the makeup off. After her fourth show here, she had gotten it down to under an hour.

Since I was in the museum, I had plenty of things to look at while Sera turned back to Blaise. Some time later, my boyfriend rounded the corner as himself, Sera packed away for another time. I gladly took the bag back, and we left to find something to eat.

"Hey, I wanted to show you something." I fished my phone out and handed it to him after unlocking it. "I want your opinion on this."

"What is it?" He took the phone, his eyes widening once he realized what he was seeing. "Is this an apartment?"

"Just a couple blocks from here. Big bedroom, massive closet, and we can turn the second bedroom into an office/costume staging area."

Blaise's big hazel eyes lifted to mine. "We?"

"Yeah."

"You want to move into an apartment with me? What about your brothers?"

"B, they'll be over all the damn time. Don't worry." I laughed. "But we need a plan together. And you need to be closer to work. I can work anywhere."

I almost dropped the bag and Blaise as he jumped up and wrapped himself around me like he had in the forest. My hands landed on his ass to hold him up, my laughing smothered by his kisses.

"I love you so much." He punctuated each word with a kiss.

"You like the apartment then?"

"Well, we'll have to see how 'massive' this closet is, but I love the gesture." He kissed me again before climbing down. "I want to have a place with you, Royal. I would love that. I just want to make sure you have your time with your family."

"Our family, baby. And we will." I tugged him to my side, his fingers laced with mine. "Now let me feed you."

The End

DEAR READER

Dear Reader,

Royal and Blaise's story is one that hits home for a lot of reasons.

Obviously, I'm very passionate about paleontology because I think you have to be to lob in jokes about dinosaur buttholes within the first couple chapters of a romance book. You also have to be a little insane and fossil crazy to cultivate an entire series based around dinosaur shifters falling in love, right?

But it's not just my love for all things dinosaurs that makes this book special to me. It's also about sexuality, expression and busting through the very strict molds around the hard sciences.

As a pansexual person myself, I love seeing more representation of my sexuality in romances. Royal is meant to be not only a celebration of geeky goodness (I also love *Yuri on Ice* and TMNT of course), but also insight in how this pansexual storm loves people. All people.

Hell, we love everyone.

Blaise's story around being the less conventional dinosaur nerd is important right now.

Within the paleo community, there is a booming growth of

identities and expressions coming to the field. The more traditional folks in academia are slowly coming around, but there are plenty who are still as unyielding as the rocks they dig up. Challenging the norm of what makes a paleontologist or even who should be allowed to be a dinosaur geek, is the main driving point behind Blaise.

He's loud, proud, and can go hiking in skirts.

Hell yes.

Basically, the moral of this story is: love what you want, who you want, and be yourself.

- Maz

ABOUT THE AUTHOR

Maz Maddox has always wanted to be an author.

Well, almost always.

At first she wanted to be a dinosaur, but that turned out to be extremely difficult. Giving up on her dreams to be a towering Allosaurus, she discovered her love for amazing stories and started writing her own.

Maybe one day she'll try the dinosaur thing again.

Follow Maz:

www.mazmaddox.com
Newsletter signup: www.mazmaddox.com/contact
mazmaddox@gmail.com

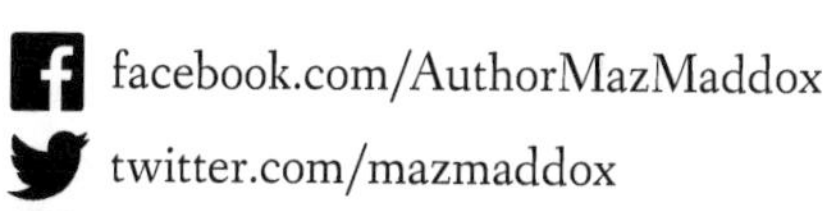

ALSO BY MAZ MADDOX

Stallion Ridge series

Heartache & Hoofbeats

Claw Marks & Card Games

Suspects & Scales

Rocks & Railways

Mimics & Mayhem

Runes, Ruin & Redemption

Fate & Fortune

RELIC series

Smash & Grab

Sink or Swim

King & Queen